T0207694

Around Brazil on the "International Adventurer"

A FICTIONAL PANEGYRIC

Mark J. Curran

Order this book online at www.trafford.com
or email orders@trafford.com

Most Trafford titles are also available at major online book retailers.

Print information available on the last page.

ISBN: 978-1-6987-0203-2 (sc)
ISBN: 978-1-6987-0202-5 (e)

Trafford rev. 07/06/2020

 www.trafford.com

North America & international
toll-free: 1 888 232 4444 (USA & Canada)
fax: 812 355 4082

This is a work of fiction written in the time of the Corona Virus. It is dedicated to those who risk their lives for all of us.

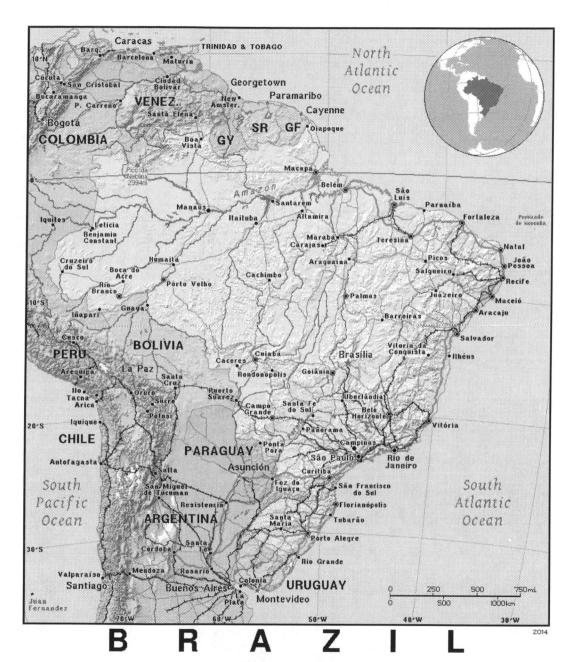

B R A Z I L

A Map of Brazil

1

AN UNEXPECTED OPPORTUNITY

I'm Mike Gaherty, a professor of language and culture at the University of Nebraska in Lincoln. Readers of my series "Letters from Brazil" already know that I teach Spanish and Portuguese, but research fortunes took me to Brazil (and the fact the senior Spanish faculty would not let go of their monopoly on the good courses of Spanish and Spanish American Literature, all rather insecure colleagues I might say). Hey, it's okay; it turned out for the best, to say the least. In most ways that is. I'm now tenured, an Associate Professor, have many terrific students and three books and some articles in reviews, all about Brazil; that means I can breathe a little more freely and enjoy teaching and work hard at what I love. If things continue as I hope, another promotion to Full Professor will happen about five years from now.

Life is not all rosy. My one-time fiancée Molly in Washington, D.C. is still not ready to reconcile after our break up a year ago, in spite of some insistent and lonely phone calls from Lincoln. She wants more time. I expect she's having too good a time in D.C. What can you do? You can't date the gorgeous, stacked co-eds I see on the mall at school, a big no-no here at the U. of N. There are a couple of good-looking young teachers in my department, and eligible, one in particular who teaches Mexican Literature who likes me but makes fun of my good but not perfect Spanish. And I've met a couple of young, cute Nebraska farm girls working in state government in Lincoln. But nothing serious, and less to write home to Mom about; she's getting antsy by the way, I'm going on 30 now.

The other "bummer" is I was "dis-invited" last summer in 1971 from returning to Brazil for research by Brazil's national security agency, the "Department of Public Security" [DOPS]. They were worried about the connection to the most popular and best in my opinion of Brazilian song writers and singers, Chico Buarque de Holanda. We are good friends and I wrote "Letters" to the "New York Times" praising his music and on-going protest of the lack of artistic freedom in the time of "pre-censorship" by the military regime in Brazil. The exit was all very cordial, and very Brazilian; the General – Head of the Censorship Board who basically kicked me out said, "We are not throwing you out of Brazil but simply suggesting you get on the next plane to New York."

I went to New York (after several goodbyes to friends including lady friends in Rio), met with James Hansen of the "New York Times," caught him up with my latest "Letter from Brazil" and worked out a plan for writing for the next year, winter of 1971 and Spring of 1972. There was a reunion with Molly later on late last Fall and a decision "to see how it goes." I've been in Lincoln ever since. I won't say it's boring because it isn't, but something is missing.

That's where the opportunity comes into the narration. It's a new year, academic year 1971 - 1972, my 4th at U of N., late Fall in Lincoln, the U. football team is doing well but not that well, 8-3, not bad for the Big 8 but like they say, "no cigar." Things however are about to change. I got a phone call out of the blue yesterday from no less than Susan Gillian, head of personnel for Adventure Travel out of Los Angeles. I had heard of them, but never paid much attention, seemed like just another of those travel companies, a dime a dozen I thought. I was wrong, way wrong. They are one of perhaps five top-flight expedition travel companies in the world. That means they want to take customers to all parts of the globe to see major sights, emphasizing nature and culture, and on small but well-equipped ships. They have a total of seven in the fleet, maybe because of the "Seven Seas" of the world. I don't know.

The culture part is where I would fit in. Susan said they are planning a trip this coming July and early August in 1972, a long one of over thirty days as an all - encompassing view of Brazil. She checked me out primarily through my book "Adventures of a 'Gringo' Researcher in Brazil in the 1960s" but more recently in the fact made fiction series of "Letters from Brazil" through the NYT publishing company (I wrote "Letters" to the "Times" for two years, later made into books). Her take: the earlier book was incredibly informative and knowledgeable and the "Letters" a lot of fun, a good "recipe" for what she was looking for: a person who could inform the AT passengers of the country they were visiting, what to see and what to expect, but not with an "egg-head" stuffy approach. I did brag a little, I think ok under the circumstances (maybe it helped get me a job), saying I had a reputation as a good lecturer and am known for my enthusiasm.

We talked a long while of my experience, my take on Brazil today, of the way the "International Adventurer," the flagship AT operates (the ship scheduled for the big Brazil trip) and what would be expected. It's a sleek modern expedition ship with the right pedigree – built at the O Porto Shipyards in O Porto and Officers from the Modern School of Navigation of Sagres. Although it travels the world it specializes in Portugal and Spain, Portugal's route around Africa to India and eventually China and Japan and over to the Americas and Brazil. Wow! Couldn't be better for my studies and interests. Oh yeah, and salary, a quite respectable retainer for five weeks' work. Susan emphasized there would be diverse duties, not just the on-board lectures, but also being present for the on-shore excursions, their "lead culture person" even though with 100 passengers, there might be three or four different excursions going on at the same time. There would almost always be at least one if not two nature excursions. An additional important duty would be spending time with the passengers during meals, conversing with them and answering any questions. I quipped that I would probably have more than they. She sent me a handbook of AT and brochures of past trips, asked me to look it all over; if I liked it, the job was mine. This all was a first for the young professor, but I surmised I should "be cool" and not too anxious to jump at the opportunity.

Susan said we would have to move expeditiously in the next month in order to include me in the snazzy colored twenty-page trip brochure. I interjected that there might be one glitch – with the "invitation" by the Department of Public Security to leave Brazil the end of last summer, I explained a visa could be a problem (I explained very briefly the interaction with Chico Buarque de Holanda, his music and protests against the government, all dealt with in "Letters III"). Both of us put our heads together and agreed that since I would not be doing research, but just doing cultural lecturing, and for a major North American Travel Company, that AT could hopefully arrange a "business visa" along with something new, a "Seaman's Card," a requirement of ship staff throughout the world. (It made me think of a song we sang in grade school, "I'd Like to Be a Pirate and Sail Upon the Sea," a song that made me think of "Treasure Island"). Geeze, that was twenty-five years ago! Susan, a veteran of all this, said she anticipated there would be no problem with the visa. There would be necessary updating of international vaccines and shots, making sure my passport was up to date (it still was, several years left until expiration). "No problem," I said, "doing research the past few years in Brazil, I am all up to date."

After reading the brochure that arrived just one day later, I got so excited I could hardly stand it, and called Susan to sign me up, trying not to seem too excited! I had read in the Handbook that there is a music specialist on board the "International Adventurer," in fact permanent staff of AT, that handles both on - shore and on – board entertainment, a top flight ethnomusicologist who travels the world with AT. She said she would put me in touch with Eli (Elijah Hamilton) to talk about any music ideas I had. Susan said the passengers tend to be middle aged to retirement age, they are the ones who can afford such trips – AT expeditions are not cheap, but the company prides itself on providing the absolute best, bar none, to its paying passengers. AT calls them all "adventurers."

It's November now and I am working hard at putting together the on-board cultural lectures, maybe as many as fifteen in all. They will hit the highlights of "An Introduction to Brazil," combine history, politics, religion, literature, folklore, and good times, meaning food, drink and Carnival, to get the folks in the mood for the on-shore excursions. Eli will ply passengers with the best of Brazilian music in the meantime (and someone in the bar will do so during cocktail hour). I also have to get them ready for each geographic area and city to be visited. I love doing all this; it is precisely what I had been studying for six years for the Ph.D. and teaching the last three. I had scanned hundreds of slides from previous travels and research and moved to CDs, so that would illustrate the talks. I learned that while at sea there are normally two lectures in the a.m., two in the p.m. and also learned that can be "iffy," dolphin and whale sightings can and do jumble the schedule. The AT expert naturalists also contribute regularly. And I forgot about the undersea diver and ocean expert. We are all instructed to mix with the passengers during the evening cocktail hour before fine dining later.

The great thing about the AT trip would be I would not miss any classes, would keep the U. of N. paychecks coming (taken on 12 months basis) and have a terrific change of pace from routine in Lincoln. There could be no formal arrangement with James Hansen and the "Times" during the trip because AT was my employer with all rights, copyrights, etc. But I could send him a long "Letter" with my own observations after the trip. Friends and even colleagues were giving me a bad time, most of them ill-informed and thinking of the normal big company cruise ships and on-board lecturers. All a bit fluffy "gig" for retirees. I was a little defensive in saying this was a lot different, like maybe undergraduate Liberal Arts compared to an intensive M.A. or even Ph.D. I would find out soon enough.

AT personnel in the home office were indeed travel specialists, and a well-oiled machine; all the preparations went like clockwork – the visa, the Sea Man's Card, and even the staff uniform, sun and bug shirts, nice polo shirts for lecture time, IA baseball style travel caps in three colors, and even a warm wooly staff jacket I guess for the sea air. When it came time to leave, all the documents had arrived safely including the stack of travel tickets on Delta Airlines, Omaha to Atlanta and the International Flight to Manaus in Brazil where I would board the ship.

As a first timer I probably could have used about one-half of what I actually packed, not knowing of the efficient laundry service on board, and maybe have geared up more – a better camera, quality but smaller; light-weight binoculars - but I had the essentials. The lecture notes and slides on CDs were in my carry-on backpack as well as all the irreplaceable travel documents. And plenty of those yellow lined notebooks and pens as well. Oh yeah, and lots of Pepto Bismol (the professor is known for his fragile stomach).

I made sure my modest bachelor apartment would be waiting for me the first of September and even called Molly to let her know what I was up to. She was excited for me, understanding that getting out of Lincoln for awhile was not all bad, and encouraged me to send some postcards or even a letter or two. No commitments but just staying in touch. I thought to myself; hmm, sounds like a repeat of Brazil last summer in 1971 and that did not turn out so bad.

2

IT ALL BEGINS, OMAHA TO ATLANTA AND ON TO MANAUS

June 29th, 1972. I don't know what other companies do, but AT sends staff to ships via business class, which in the final analysis boosts morale and good will for sure. And maybe a little more sleep. I had always been in coach on all my previous flights, and even then, when on Varig the Brazilian National Airline the in-flight service and food were terrific. I would say Delta business class matched it. This meant two seats on the side of the aisle, a larger seat and more leg room and nice Delta service particularly on the international flight. The four-hour flight from Omaha to Atlanta passed fairly quickly. It was seven hours from Atlanta to Manaus, but the flight left at midnight and arrived in Manaus at 7:00 a.m. Brazil time. We would have Delta's version of Brazilian demitasse coffee ("cafezinho"), croissants and orange juice as a wake-me-upper before landing. It must have been one of those turn-around flights because they had the local papers, just one day old, from Rio and São Paulo ("O Globo" and "A Folha de São Paulo"). No big headlines out of the ordinary as far as I could see, politics – President Garrastazu Médici's on-going big "pharaonic projects" in the works, the Itaipu Dam and the Trans-Amazonic Highway, no elections or campaign stories (there were none to be had in the military's governing plan for the present), cool weather and rain in store for Rio and São Paulo (but not the Amazon) and preliminaries for the World Cup in 1974.

June 30th. The Lockheed L - 1011 gradually nosed down, heading lower, and we could see the Amazon Rain Forest and what seemed like river after river before easing onto the concrete runway of the Manaus International Airport. AT had their agent in the airport lobby with the "Gaherty" sign, and more importantly, all my documents for getting on the ship the next day.

An aside, the Manaus Airport was now truly international due to the city's huge growth as the center of the Brazilian "Free Trade Zone" and new manufacturing area, the national flights terminal adjacent to our terminal a sight to see with the hustle and bustle of all the Brazilians arriving with huge empty suitcases to load up on TVs, tape recorders, cameras, and all kinds of electronics to take back to the rest of Brazil tax free! It was altogether different from the small - city and tropical lazy atmosphere when I was first there in 1967.

AT had also arranged the transportation to the hotel from their chauffer - agent, a part-time lawyer "in between jobs," and he offered to drive me around town that day. I said I'd see. The "International Adventurer" or "Adventurer" as everyone calls it would not be in until the next day, so I was put up in the very upscale Hotel Tropical on the outskirts of the city, located adjacent to the Rio Negro and would have the full day for resting up and seeing what I could of Manaus. The city for me had vivid but limited memories, a longer than planned stay in research days in the 1960s when with a very limited budget on Brazilian Tariff III fares I had a hard time getting a flight out of the city back along the Amazon River to Belém do Pará and then on to Fortaleza in the Northeast. See the map. However, I had spent three full days in Manaus in 1967 making use of every minute – walking and seeing all the dock area including the famous floating dock on pontoons, the market or fair along the river bank, the dozens if not hundreds of passenger, cargo and ferry boats on this huge river port, the zoo with the "Coca-Cola" water and dying animals and sloth on the bus, the famous Opera House and an all-day ride to the local rivers on the "Milk Boat." I wrote about all that in "Adventures" and that was responsible in part for Susan Gillian's enthusiasm to get me on board for this trip.

Unofficial Greeter, Hotel Tropical

What a difference in accommodations from student days to now – the Hotel Tropical was first-class in every way with a terrific location, the swimming pools and outside gardens and zoo, I might add, overlooking the Rio Negro. I was practically in awe in what I was seeing, worth a few words, or maybe many.

Driftwood, Rosewood Woodwork

The huge lobby, adjacent dining room and wide corridors were all decorated in dark tropical woods, with beautiful pieces of what I imagined were drift wood from the River. Large paintings of tropical forest scenes – flora and fauna - adorned the walls. There was even a glassed-in area with two snowy herons, turtles, tropical plants and orchids. My room was a trifle small, but hey, just fine. Once again all in tropical hardwoods, a ceiling fan I put to good use, luxurious towels, bathrobe for the swimming pool, but funny, no TV. Huh?

Pool with Veranda Overlooking the River

Then I went outside, the Lincoln boy had never seen anything like that: a huge round swimming pool in two sections, one with a waterfall leading to the next. Deck chairs and tables and a trio at one end playing soft Bossa Nova Music. To the side of this area was a long white wall with arches, and on the other side between the thick vegetation one could see the Rio Negro (more on it in a while). Beyond this area was what they called "the gardens," manicured lawn and small kiosks everywhere with magnificent Macaws in each, all in brilliant yellow, blue, red and green. One could see the outside of the hotel's rooms, and on the upper floors, hammocks strung on the balconies. Wow! I would get back out to that area that evening, but more to do now.

After the two flights and airline food the previous day (I'm not complaining), I was hungry and was treated to a full delightful Brazilian breakfast in the beautiful dining room of five different kinds of tropical juices, pineapple, scrambled eggs and bacon, delicious coconut flavored bread, and that national mainstay – delicious chocolate or regular pound cake. And of course, Brazil's without par "café com leite." That ought to hold me, right?

There was no real jet lag, so after the big breakfast, I decide it would be off on my own to see the downtown, taking advantage of the free day. There was a surprise as I was walking out the main door of the hotel lobby to catch the hotel van to the city. A fellow in a white linen suit, a black string tie, and a straw fedora. Uh oh, I had seen this before many times in Brazil! And sure enough he came over, offered a handshake and pulled out a billfold with a badge, a Department of Public Safety [DOPS] man, the main agent in Manaus. "Oi, professor Gaherty! I'm Odálio Martines, and I've been told to greet you and bring you up to date with official matters you might want to keep in mind during your stay in Brazil. We are of course linked to all coming and going, and when the request for your visa to be renewed came, a red flag went up. There's a great ice cream shop inside the hotel, it's hot as usual, and I'll buy you an açai ice cream, the best there is!"

This was an invitation not to be turned down, so I agreed, shaking my new DOPS' friend hand and saying lead the way. The shop was right off that beautiful lobby with tropical hardwood décor. There were many small tables with chairs where we plunked down after getting the large, I daresay, scoops of açaí. It was Brazilian style – cups with a tiny spoon – not that "barbaric" gringo way of just licking the cone. Odálio was up to date and did not miss a beat. "Professor, or if I can just call you Miguel? (sorry, we have a pisser joke with that name in Brazil; when a Brazilian man has to take a pee, he says 'Vou falar com Miguel' ['I've got to talk to Mike!']. Ha ha ha. Or maybe you would prefer 'Arretado' – your reputation precedes you." I interjected, "You guys certainly didn't waste any time. I'm a bit surprised to meet you, but the pleasure is mine." We both laughed.

Odálio took the floor, as it were, and continued. "Miguel, we have not forgotten last year's exodus and advice to you about not returning, but 'Adventure Travel' is one stud of a company and brings lots of bucks to Brazil. If the travelers have a good time, spend some money, and have good things to say about our wonderful country, that certainly is welcomed. That my friend is why we granted your visa, in spite of last year. Lecturing and pointing out the positive aspects of Brazil can do no harm, and since you **definitely** will not be doing research, we can welcome you. But we will be keeping an eye on you and your itinerary. Chuckle. AT's Expedition ships are not known for bringing secret agents to Brazil. And hey, it might not be a bad idea to invite agents such as myself on board for a tour and a drink. That would do wonders!"

"Senhor Odálio, just a note for you, I am a 'rookie' on board, a first -timer, and I certainly want to do my best and impress the company and show them they have not made a mistake so I'll be minding my p's and q's for sure. I'm not sure they would be comfortable with the Brazilian equivalent of the FBI snooping about the ship or its passengers, but maybe we can figure out a good PR move. I'll have to let you know; I haven't even been on the ship yet. I'm thinking some kind of a courtesy visit for let's say, the National Commission of Tourism. Can you guys swing that?"

"Você deveria estar brincando? ["You must be kidding?"]. Hey Miguel, that was only **my** idea, just a whim or maybe a joke. I like your 'jeito' [quick thinking arrangement] however. What's on tap for today? And do you need any company?"

"Odálio, this is one of those rare times when I'd like to go on my own. I have 'saudades' of my visit here in 1967 and would just like to bum around to some places for old times' sake, but it's all tourism."

"Fine, but some advice, get yourself a good sun hat, and we always walk in the shade when there is some. You'll be surprised that there is often a cool breeze coming from the river. Manaus is known for many shady characters with the smuggling trade at its highest in Brazil (along with Ciudad del Este in Paraguay near Iguaçu Falls). This is in spite of the so-called 'Free Zone' and in fact is probably caused by it. There just aren't enough government employees to watch everything, and believe it or not, there is more than one way to get out of Manaus. We can't check the hundreds of small passenger boats that come and go every day. Let me give you my card with a phone number. It goes to the downtown office but I always check in regularly. It might accidentally get you out of any scrapes. Foreigners are filet mignon to the pickpockets and muggers here and you don't exactly look Brazilian."

We parted on those terms and I started what began as an amazing day of tourism, but constantly thinking of my previous days and the scrapes I got into down near the docks. The "Adventurer" would be in the next day and was not scheduled to leave for two more days after that, so I figured some of my tourism would be duplicated, but I wasn't yet apprised of schedule and places, so did not want to take a chance to miss a few things.

I took the hotel van down to the wharf, walked around the outside market on planks over the water at the edge of the river (still noting the huge stacks of vegetables and fruit, including all the bananas, maybe still with those tarantulas they talk about), and on up to the old fish market enclosed in beautiful steel décor modeled after the Santa Isabel Elevator in Lisbon and maybe, if not a tourist exaggeration, done by the designer of the Eiffel Tower. You have to remember; this is not the Amazon; that is several kilometers out of Manaus when the Rio Negro meets the Solimões coming down from Peru and Ecuador. But the Rio Negro looks like a small ocean. It's funny, the main thing that came back to me was the smell of it all, docks, mud and fish market. On the wall up from the river and market there were numbers to mark high and low water marks, a 70-foot difference between them. Below the fish market you could see dozens if not hundreds of local cargo, passenger and ferry boats, all plying the Rio Negro, the Solimões, and the hundreds of tributaries. The entrance to the dock where the big river freighters and, I surmise, the "Adventurer" would tie up was blocked off, a barrier in front with one of those telephone booth sized guard houses, but you could see the huge pontoons still supporting the dock floors. We were still close to high "tide" from the winter rains and the Rio Negro seemed to stretch for at least a couple of miles to the south; one could see lots of debris including huge logs in the current.

You just basically walked across the street from the market area and you were in the middle of a prosperous Brazilian commercial downtown, the streets crowded with all kinds of shoppers. The noise was deafening with each shop blaring out its wares or "mood music" to attract the shoppers (and pretty sales girl "greeters" for the same reason). The shops were full of that Free Zone "stuff," and that's a good word for it, endless camera shops, watch shops with Rolex knockoffs! TVs, appliances, and gadgets. And lots of leather goods. And fishing rods, reels and accessories. I was jostled hard coming out of a record store, glared at the guy and he ran; fortunately, belongings were in a money belt, and I only carried xerox copies of my passport and visa in my shirt or he would have had them. I prided myself for never having been mugged in Brazil; this came close. Porra! Odálio was right!

Travel and over night flight were catching up with me, and also thinking that AT would surely have the Opera House on the local schedule, so I caught a taxi back to the Hotel Tropical, took a quick shower and went for a swim, still allowing a quick nap before hotel cocktail hour (with regional goodies) and dinner. There was a call from Waldo the AT representative saying that the "Adventurer" would indeed be in during the night and I could board at 10 the next morning.

There was one moment of interest later that day at the hotel's cocktail hour at 6 p.m. I was anxious to continue getting back to Portuguese and out by the pool had worked up a conversation with a gentleman who turned out to be a civil engineer, specialist in soils, soil mechanics, and a consultant to the "Departamento Nacional de Infraestrutura e Transporte" [DNIT], The National Road Building Ministry, in charge of the North Region. Over a couple of real and not "national" scotch whiskies (Johnny Walker Red), something Engineer Fred Sabbatine wanted to emphasize to me in the "New Brazil," we had a great conversation. He could answer every question I had on the planned but just under construction, new "Trans - Amazon Highway" [A Transamazônica], probably the most famous and ambitious of the Military Government's "big" projects, in fact the latest one it was staking its reputation on. I had researched and written about it in "Letters III" and if the reader recalls, was almost on a trip to João Pessoa with Chico Buarque to give a concert "celebrating" the inauguration and early phases of the massive project. When I mentioned this, Fred almost yelling, exclaimed, "Porra, rapaz!" saying he actually had heard about that. He looked at me a moment, looked again and said "Você mesmo é o 'Arretado'?" ["Are you the 'Cool Guy' himself?"] From then on, he was pouring the drinks, and I had to say "Chega" ["Enough"] when he wanted to fill the glasses with straight whiskey! He was a huge fan of Chico Buarque's from "A Banda" all the way to some recent "dangerous" songs (he winked and said, "Não conte a ninguém!" ["Don't tell anyone."] He said his daughter had a contraband copy of the "Mistakes of Our Youth" album).

Like a good Brazilian he wanted to know what I was doing in Brazil, invited me to dinner (and there would have been more, "extra-curricular" activities in the local "zone" if I had agreed). We spent two hours outside on the veranda by the pool with cool Bossa Nova music and aforesaid scotch talking about Brazil, a fortuitous re-introduction to the country for me. What was great was I got what amounted to an "insider's" synopsis of the state of the country. Fred was currently in Manaus checking out the north-south, Manaus - Porto Velho Highway Project that would intersect with the Transamazon Highway at Humaitá several hundred miles south of Manaus traversing a maze of rivers and dense forest. It was in the surveying stage only. What I told him was that I would have a big day tomorrow, joining the staff of the "International Adventurer" on a 30-day coastal expedition of Brazil. He wanted all the details and I could tell he would have loved to have been aboard. "Porra! Rapaz! You are going so see more of Brazil than some of our bigwig politicians!"

He wanted to know my role and when I told him he promised to get every one of my books and invited me more than once to come visit him and the family at their ocean front condo in Santos (one learns in Brazil that being invited once may be a courtesy or even just being nice, but more than once is probably a serious invitation). The main residence was in Brasília but he said, "Unless Tio Sam pulls off that flooding of the Amazon trick, your ship won't get **there**!" And he laughed and laughed, "An old leftist joke from the 60s." I didn't tell him I heard it from the leftist students in Recife in 1967, but they were serious – the U.S. CIA was going to flood the Amazon and make it an "American ocean!"

What was learned about the highway? Progress was just getting started, slow, with plans to plow through the backlands of Paraíba State, really the easy part; the backlands "desert" [sertão] had dried clay soil that could be dealt with before laying asphalt. But then the plan would change – dealing with the savannah forest to the west and then the actual beginning of rain forest in southern Maranhão State and for sure in Pará. Fred was no dummy and not naïve either; he was quite aware of the obstacles ahead – mainly rainy season with up to 150 inches of rain a year, stopping all progress in a huge mudhole, then a sweltering tropical hell of heat baking the ruts in the road construction, and the worst – the fluctuations in temperature, moisture, sun light, all affecting asphalt.

He tried one more time to get me to go along to the red-light zone, winking at me and saying, "Você não é um daqueles veados?" I assured him that was not the case but that we would have to have a rain check on the late-night socializing. I mentioned the same type of "relax," the Historic Mansion along the beach in Flamengo in Rio and my lady friend Maria Aparecida (Lindalva) working there and he about fell on the floor – "I know that beauty! Expensive but what a lay!" So, we called it a night with promises of staying in touch and me calling him for sure in Santos.

I was asleep when my head hit the pillow, but not before hearing the message on the room answering machine: AT's man, Waldo, would meet me in the hotel lobby tomorrow at 10:00 a.m. and take me to the ship! I'd have to get up at 7:00 and be sure all my stuff was together and ready to leave the room, not forgetting anything, no small order.

3

PROFESSOR, YOU'VE LIVING A DREAM! – THE "INTERNATIONAL ADVENTURER"

July 1ˢᵗ. Waldo was right on time, walking into the lobby of the Hotel Tropical with a large attaché case in which he assured me were all my documents – the Passport (with the Brazilian Visa in place), International Health Card, Sea Man's Card. I was not used to trusting anybody with all that stuff, in fact never before, but Waldo laughed, assured me AT hadn't lost one yet! The desk clerks waved goodbye, complimenting me on my Portuguese, one of the girls suddenly realizing and shouting, "O' gente, é o Arretado, o amigo de Chico Buarque!" We took about five minutes, they all wishing they had known sooner, apologizing for the "poor" tourist treatment I had received, saying there would have been an upgrade! "A próxima vez talvez, hein?"

It didn't take long for the air-conditioned taxi to get down to the port where we pulled up to a tiny office the size of a telephone booth with a large iron barrier to the side and steel mesh fence on either side of that. Beyond the booth was the steel walkway on top of the pontoons and the big dock. My guy Waldo and the customs agent were in a long conversation, which got a little heated. Waldo told me they claimed they didn't have my name on their list (An aside to me, "Foda! A burocracia aqui nunca acaba!")" ["F***! There is no end to the bureaucracy here!"] It happens all the time in Brazil, you're in a situation where you could swear it was the first time the government official in charge ever had to do that procedure, even though it was probably the thousandth time! I could write (and in fact did) about the customs' employees ["Agentes da Alfandega"] in the major airports. You've heard of the old-fashioned rubber stamp?

With the car windows down to "negotiate" the procedure, we were finally "liberated" as they say in Brazil. Waldo said, "Pois é, Arretado. A gente se despede aqui." So, we hauled my large suitcase and good-sized pack out of the trunk and Waldo gave me a big "abraço" and "Boa Viagem." I slung the pack to my back, picked up the bag and walked twenty yards toward the river and turned the corner and there it was! The "International Adventurer!" Nossa! It was more beautiful than even the pictures in the brochures – an incredibly sleek, snow-white, small by ocean cruise ship standards expedition ship! It was hot, I was sweating like crazy, no time to lollygag looking at the ship. The metal stairway up from the dock was open and a uniformed officer (in pressed white shorts, sneakers and short sleeved white shirt and officer's white cap) was waiting for me. He wasn't worried about papers (I'm sure they were on the phone to the Manaus Customs people), but grabbed the suitcase and said, "Professor Mike, follow me."

Up the ramp, inside to the right was an elevator, the door open and we both walked in, but with little room to spare. He said, "Professor Gaherty, we've been expecting you. Welcome aboard. I'm the executive officer Martim Mendes. I understand you speak Portuguese, 'Bemvindo a bordo.' I hope you can adapt to our continental accent! But all shipboard activity is in English." The door opened, we were on level three, plush dark wooden walls, deep carpets, and soon to n. 323. The cabin door was unlocked, he carried the big suitcase inside and I followed. He said, "Make yourself comfortable, a nice cool shower if you want, and I'll meet you for lunch in the chart room below the Captain's Bridge and give you the quick "cook's tour" afterwards. (He gave me instructions to find it and I only got lost once.) It's standard procedure; you will be a little familiar with the ship before cocktails at 5:30 where you will meet many of the staff and crew and perhaps a few passengers, and then meet more passengers at dinner. Oh, we call them 'adventurers.' By the way, enjoy your accommodations. Susan Gillian pulled a little rank to get you into adventurer quarters, said you would be more comfortable and not so grouchy. Ha."

It turned out that most adventurers would be flying in during the day and in effect we all would meet for cocktails and then dinner, and I would learn, an intense two-days of exploring tomorrow and the next day. So Martim warned me it would be a bit helter-skelter and we would run into folks settling in. Even though it was now about 11:00 a.m. the tropics had got to me waiting to board and the shower felt terrific. Refreshed, I found my way to the chart room toward the bow, looking out over the observation deck. That morning it was used for a general staff meeting, and as fate would have it, I was the only new staff member aboard, introduced and applauded by a friendly group of astounding people. I'll mention many, but some will just come up as the expedition evolves.

Captain "Tony" Antônio Guimarães, with the "Adventurer" since its maiden expedition in 2004, he a veteran of the Portuguese High Sea School of Navigation in Sagres, one of the most famous historically in the world; the hotel manager Gino Amato; Joana Oliveira the purser (she would be totally the stereotype of work and efficiency and expected the same of all staff). Other officers, some on the bridge, others manning the "guts" of the ship and engines (called the denizens of the depths) would be introduced later, one a ruddy, rotund person you would rarely see, and that only on the zodiac departure deck with stairways leading to the engine room - João Tavares. Dining staff and laundry room and cabin attendants, all from Thailand would also be known.

The main people in charge of liaison with the adventurers, talks and on shore excursions were full-time employees by AT and had been all over the world. Steve Barber was AL, Adventure Leader, in charge of the itinerary and in fact, everything. But the heavy labor job involved his assistant Amy Carrier Assistant Adventure Leader [AAL] in charge of coordinating with the Brazilians (Ha! She said) for on-shore excursions, but also assigning personnel from staff as group leaders, naturalists who would double as zodiac drivers (i.e. "hot rodders") and the rest. The fly in the ointment was Brazil, always in a state of flux or with unexpected demands for the ship and AT (mainly fees, surcharges, salary and tips for local guides, many in this case since we would have around ten on-shore stops). Amy and I fortunately hit it off (and more), she having done a business residency at the Fundação Getúlio Vargas in Rio de Janeiro after a degree in Hotel Management at Cornell and knew a lot of Portuguese. She said 95 per cent of the Brazilian contacts claimed they knew English, but their definition of it and hers were different. And incidentally she was ravishingly good looking with a great build; all the naturalists loved to hang around her desk in the Staff Office on the Mud Deck, maybe just to get a peak at her blouse from above. How do I know this? Martim had told me. "You will have lots of questions, and everyone will be pleased to answer them, but they are also quite busy. You will need to do the asking, and, just keep your eyes open!"

I was overwhelmed, particularly when the naturalists - photography experts were introduced. There would be three specializing in birds, animals and plants of Brazil and one raucous guy who would handle oceanic matters, the river denizens and any diving. I would be the main guy for Brazilian culture, history and politics, no small order; one naturalist said, "I hope you've got your **** together; it's a huge task, but hey we can always talk about parrots and macaws." Jack Bataldi was the on-board ornithologist with a bird list of many thousands, over half the species on the planet, quite familiar with birds of Brazil and he would lead the birding trips. He had that degree from Cornell and twenty years' experience all over the planet. Buck Weylander was younger but with ten years on AT ships, spotting from the bow for seabirds and sea life (he had grown up on the coast of California, studied with an internship at the famous oceanic aquarium in Newport, Oregon). He would amaze with talks on whales, sharks, dolphins and a myriad of seabirds, all while on-board, and knew the fish and denizens of the Amazon we might sight. Kelly Corrigan out of Oregon State was the botanist and could name and identify hundreds of tropical plants, flowers and the insects and animals depending upon them. We would find she could gush and get excited over a butterfly. Finally, Willie "the Joker" Walsh was our divemaster, his main attribute being he was unafraid of running into big fish, barracuda, sharks and even Orcas on AT's expedition voyages throughout the world (he would meet a new one in Brazil – the "pirarucu" in Amazon rivers and running up to eight feet in length). His growing up days were in landlocked Arizona but with days and months spent on the Bay of California and its Baja Research Center at Puerto Peñasco in Baja California where he did hundreds of dives. Experience on the ships the last eight years had expanded expertise to much of the planet. The other attribute – being clever, full of jokes, you never knew for awhile when he was serious and if what he was saying was the same. A character. One other full – timer staffer was Harry Downing, jack of all trades, AT in the North Atlantic, Ship Librarian and above all, Historian. Harry could give you an hour's lecture in the King's English on most any given country in the world and its history, anything on the world-wide routes of AT. Sardonic, a bit sarcastic, but tempered by that understated English humor, Harry never failed to both entertain and educate. He did welcome my expertise on Brazil from the very beginning, but said he could handle at-sea eclectic matters. Yes. Of course.

And most important to me was Eli (Elijah) our onboard entertainment and music czar, also in charge of bringing local talent on board or arranging private performances for all of us on shore. He traveled the world collecting music, meeting local musicians and compiling a huge catalogue of talent. He and I would really hit it off, both of us huge fans of Brazilin folk and popular music. More later on our parleying to get some of my entertainer friends involved.

Steve told me after the lunch that he would need me to do the first talk tomorrow evening to prep everyone for Manaus itself, the excursion planned to the docks and fair, the water traffic, the enclosed market and the Opera House. He would schedule it during cocktail hour the next day, called

CC – Cocktails and Chat. Nothing was needed from me during that day because it would all be on the water to the Solimões, the Amazon, a hike in the jungle, a canoe trip and to a village to see the collection of raw rubber; the naturalists would have it all in hand. But I was feeling tense about the first presentation and would spend most of the evening until late hours getting the first lecture ready, coordinating with Willie who ran the apparatus for the talks from the podium in the lounge. I should not have worried; he had it all under control and would have the whole thing, microphone, DVD with images all ready for the screens throughout the lounge.

After that overwhelming lunch (I mean meeting all those people) Officer Mendes showed up right on schedule for my "ship's tour." It was so fast (not for him) that it was a blur. Here's what I remember, not in great detail. The absolute top of the ship is full of antennae. Below that deck is a glassed-in section where there is a tiny library and observation deck, a small sun deck and fitness room and sauna on the other end. Then, the all-important Bridge Deck and a few of the "higher end" cabins, some with balconies. Then upper deck with the lounge and sun deck to one end and cabins to the other end. Then the Main Deck with the dining room and more cabins. Below that the mud deck, for getting on and off, equipment for snorkeling and diving, and the laundry, and tiny shared cabins for the staff. So, there were five decks including antennae, but the bottom one almost to water level. On the outside there is a large area up front at the bow for wildlife observation, another small area on the deck below and in front of the bridge and of course the back deck adjacent to the lounge and walkways on either side. "By the time one does a 30-day trip you will see it all and use most of it."

I would have about three hours before cocktails and meeting adventurers so I spent the time preparing the first talk on Manaus, its history and importance, and the sights we would see in the down town – the wharf, docks, local traffic, huge market, enclosed Fish Market, and then the Opera House, the aforementioned items in the a.m. 9 to 11, the Opera House from 2 - 4.

4

LET IT BEGIN! COCKTAILS AND MEETING EVERONE

Most all of us gathered in the lounge on Deck III at 5:30, that included ship captain and assistants, AT Staff and adventurers (I told them all "aventureiro" sounded cool in Portuguese). Captain Antônio and Steve Barber would introduce their respective people as everyone enjoyed beverages, all "top shelf" with this outfit. The lounge was of course air conditioned, but still warm (we are in the deep tropics), so I wore an AT polo shirt, khakis, and sneakers and noticed most of the AT Staff did the same. Captain's folks were all in summer tropic whites. The adventurers seemed to be dressed, let's say, in "classy casual" I'll call it. One thing helpful for me to know was that all had seen and perused the AT Brochure for the trip and many had purchased my book "Adventures of a 'Gringo' Researcher in Brazil in the 1960s – In Search of 'Cordel.'" First time I've mentioned that, much more later; "cordel" refers to the folk popular literature of Brazil's northeast, pamphlets like broadsides, in verse, but telling stories from fiction and also like a newspaper for the common man. It was my research specialty since graduate school. Everyone will not only be familiar with it but may be sick of it by the time we get to Rio. So, they knew about me as well as all the staff, some in surprising detail.

On the other hand, I knew nothing about them - all 102, the ship full to capacity. It did not take long to discover that they indeed were more familiar with AT Travel and the IA ship than I, most all returnees from previous trips. Some will enter this narration as time goes by. Suffice to say they were from all walks of life, most in early retirement, from the business world, government service (big jobs in some cases), doctors, lawyers, accountants and even university professors, researchers and presidents. And I mean both men and women. A few would be "self-made" up from your bootstraps folks, from modest backgrounds but wealthy and successful today. (They might have been the most interesting.) One was a daredevil, car racing back home, anything dangerous. And there was a smidgen of famous people, from the music world and the arts. Wow! I thought, any farmers? Surprisingly yes, found out later. The common denominator or denominators – they could afford the $32,000 per person price of the trip, wanted to see more of the world, loved nature, and were insatiably curious which would keep all of us on our toes.

Most common question to me: Why did you get interested in Brazil? And how did you learn Portuguese? The compliments would come soon enough as I was needed to translate on-shore and used some Portuguese in the on-board talks. I found out they were testing me, in effect, checking me out. That might have been the case with the first conversation, brief as it was, with Amy the AAL. Dark brown hair, a sparkle in her green eyes, about 5 ft. 7 and curves in all the right places. And as I would learn, as impressive intellectually as she was physically. I was sitting at one of the bar stools in the lounge, revolving to take in as much as I could but reticent yet to say much, when she came up, stuck out her hand and said, "Oi Miguel, ou talvez devo dizer Bemvindo Arretado! Já fiquei sabendo de suas peripécias com Chico Buarque o ano passado. Uma surpresa vendo você agora. Isso requer explicação!" ["Hi Michael, or perhaps I should say 'Welcome Arretado'! I already know of your shenanigans with Chico Buarque last year. It is a surprise to see you now. There has got to be an explanation!] I was shocked for a moment at the beautiful carioca accent

I had just heard, but made a quick recovery, mumbling something like "Que mais há de dizer? Precisei voltar ao Brasil!" ["What can I say? I needed to get back to Brazil!"] From that moment on I don't think I could get enough of Amy. She said she had to circulate but maybe we could get together soon at the informal breakfast group of staff outside the dining room. First I heard of that. "Aren't we supposed to have all the meals with the adventurers?" She laughed, "You'll see enough of them, and I'm the busiest person (ahem, cough cough) on the ship, so you better not miss me!"

"I've got the message and it's my pleasure. You can count on it."

Introductions went as planned taking up most of an hour with polite applause for everyone. Willie stole the show when he was introduced, doing a summersault and backflip in the center of the lounge next to the speaker's podium. Everyone howled, he bowed and on we went. It ended with Steve's welcome and the plan for tomorrow; all of us together at first on the two-decker "Amazon Dreamer" tour boat on the Rio Negro until the confluence with the Solimões to form the Amazon, a chance to see the famous pink dolphins, then to shore for a "jungle hike" and a canoe ride through one of the famous "igarapés" or jungle streams and drinks and snacks at the "Jungle Lodge" a subsidiary of the Hotel Tropical. The main question by someone, "What do we wear?" Steve laughed and said "Your best butterfly catcher imitation! Sun and bug shirt and pants, sneakers, a good sun hat and maybe insect repellant (although we'll have that). And rain gear, always! The water bottle from your room, and above all don't forget your cameras and binocs!" All was running late so we were hustled out of the lounge (after my learning all of us on staff were expected to help pick up) and headed in to dinner.

I might add this was not the usual semi-dress Captain's welcome; that would come the first night "at sea" on the Amazon. Because of the tidying up of the lounge we staff were late getting to the dining room, and passengers had already chosen their spots, many of them knowing each other. I spotted a table of six with four seats taken, I asked if I could join them and was welcomed. It turned out to be two retired professors from the

University of California in San Diego, both with research interests in Latin America, one in Mexican history the other in political science of the entire region; their wives Wanda and Jackie just as talented and with academic credentials as well. John and Cliff had spent time mainly in the Spanish-speaking countries but were very familiar with Brazil, so we could relate and share experiences. I can't name it but there was a local dish, some kind of a fish stew with wonderful vegetables, açaí and coconut ice cream for dessert. And I discovered a favorite of the region, Brazilian Xingú dark beer, not heavy but served icy cold! The Xingu River is one of the main tributaries of the Amazon.

After dinner it was back to the cabin with a lot more polishing of my first talk, the introduction to Manaus tomorrow evening. It had to get done because I would not dare miss tomorrow's outing in the waters of the Amazon.

5

AMAZON DREAMING

Dreamer Tour Boat, Rio Negro

July 2nd. We were all awakened via the intercom call at 5:30 a.m., Steve the AL telling of the plans for the day - early breakfast at 6:00 a.m., everyone to the mud deck at 7:00, down the stairway to the dock, and a short walk to one of the local tourist ferries the "Amazon Dreamer." It was two decks with lots of observation space up front and along the sides. People were pretty good about sharing observation space, at times with gentle urging by staff. It was a good thirty minutes moving fast via the large diesel engine, almost gliding along what I like to call the "Coca-Cola" waters of the Rio Negro.

Willie and the local guides kept us all informed, a non-stop lesson on river ecology, Willie noting that we would see perhaps 100 species of Amazon fish tomorrow in the huge fish market, most dead, and with some luck, a few live ones today. The Rio Negro in itself is a huge river, the largest black-water river in the world, a significant contributor to the waters of the Amazon at 13 per cent of its total volume. It looked like black tea or Coca-Cola to me seeing it for the first time in a small tributary running through the Manaus Zoo back in 1967. The color comes from tannins, or decayed vegetation along the banks. It was thought the river and its acidic water would not allow fish, but studies have shown that in the entire course of the river from Colombia, touching Venezuela and its long journey to Manaus it may support as many as 700 fish species. But Manaus locals deny this, claiming if you want to see real fishing go to the Solimões or the Amazon itself. Whatever the case, the naturalists got into quite a discussion about it; it took a full thirty minutes at full speed out of Manaus to reach our first destination and the most famous – the meeting of the waters – where the Rio Negro joins the muddy, yellow Solimões from the west to form the real Amazon.

The best view is from the air and I saw it years ago, but even in the ferry you could see the significant color change, the mixing of the near-black Rio Negro with the yellow and then the two forming the muddy Amazon miles downstream. The currents of both caused this we were told. The tourist attraction is pink dolphins, as amazing as that might seem. The fact is that this dolphin is in the entire Amazon River Basin, in the rivers of six countries, with the local name of "boto" and with many indigenous legends about it. We did indeed see perhaps one-half dozen of the dolphins (they are in the whale family as Willie would let us know). One close call, an unnamed passenger, but soon to be known to all, extra ambitious in wanting photos with his 20 inch long camera lens, was bending way over the bow, the boat hit a wave (yes there are large waves particularly where the waters mix, not a good place for a swim) and if it were not for Willie and a "Dreamer" guide grabbing his belt and shoes he would have been overboard, and probably a goner in the current. Unfortunately, he did not learn from his mistake and we all soon were counseled to keep an eye on him on all on-shore excursions. In fact, it became quite a joke as to whom would be designated "on duty" to keep an eye on him. It even earned him a staff nickname - Wonky.

After the "Encontro das Águas" we continued for a good forty minutes to the south shore of the Solimões where there was a make shift dock, basically planks and a wooden stairway with rope guides about waist high. We were divided into four groups, the first early out after snacks on board the "Dreamer" and then the others phased in every fifteen minutes. The wait was not unpleasant; you could nap in one of the hammocks, listen to the piped in local music trio on deck, or just watch the flow of the river, many birds about and lots of river traffic. Everyone seemed happy; this was the real thing! Including a surprisingly cool breeze coming off the huge river.

That changed as soon as we walked up the wooden ramp and onto a trail that climbed gradually about seventy feet before it leveled off, the river in view to one side. Then we did a sudden left and were in the Amazon Rain Forest! Humidity climbed, everything seemed wet and we were soaked in sweat. Kelly Corrigan was in our group and was talking non-stop identifying plants, terrific bromeliads she says! What was missing from my very limited knowledge and experience were the huge Amazon "umbrella" trees capable of 100 to 200 feet in height with a huge trunk. The "Dreamer" guide said, "Unfortunately anything close to the river was cut down years ago, in some cases up to 100 years ago. Those trees still grow but far from the river. Most of the early buildings in Manaus were hewed from their logs." After about thirty minutes we arrived to a very large opening in the forest and came to what I would call a lake. The guide said yes and no, in reality a very large igarapé or fresh water stream feeding into a lake. At one end was the "Jungle Lodge" we were promised. We walked on a well-built sturdy walkway – bridge to a quaint and really pretty thatched, conical lodge with a deck all the way around, tables all set and waiters in "tropical" uniform of shorts, shirt and sandals.

We were offered icy cold bottled water, soft drinks including Brazil's most popular – Guaraná - or an icy beer. Most all just took the water, although I pushed them a little to try Brazil's "Coca-Cola" high sugar, high caffeine drink. Then they put us in long dugout canoes ("like the natives use") and gave us a thirty-minute ride through the igarapé.

Lilly Pads and Alligator

Kelly was ecstatic particularly about the huge "Vitória Regina" water lillies, maybe four feet across. We thought we saw a small Brazilian alligator ("jacaré," in the caiman or alligator family) resting on one. The trip through the lagoon and igarapé was indeed beautiful, thick foliage and then suddenly brilliant flashes of blue – the huge Blue Morpho Butterflies endemic to the Amazon Basin. Kelly had a net, caught one and showed us all the color close up, explaining more than we needed to know about them (more to be seen in the tourist market to the side of the fish market in Manaus). We were told we could go for a swim but no one took them up on it, some Adventurers I thought! I did ask the guide if there were piranhas here and was told no. For what it's worth, and that's not much, I was told if you have good current, no piranhas. That was in 1967 when I was on the riverboat on the São Francisco River in Minas Gerais and Bahia, and then was shown piranhas in the fish market along the river. Hmm. We joked about putting our fingers or hand in the water to cool it off. What's Randy Travis's song? "On the other hand, was a golden band." Gulp. We were told that at night there was a good chance to at least hear if not see a "jaguar."

After a lunch of fish stew the rest of the p.m. was a stop or two along the river, at one place an indigenous village where they still tapped rubber trees (an entire other topic for later) and gave a demonstration of the same, and the ride back "home" passing floating gas stations and past the old famous floating "favela" on the outskirts or Manaus where they filmed "Our Man in Rio" with Jean Paul Belmondo back in the 1950s (I would ask Harry to get it for the ship library). In the movie it was full of drug runners, narcotics smugglers, prostitutes, gamblers and plain ole' thieves. I read that the Brazilian government burns it down every few years for good measure (offering the denizens cheap shacks in the interior but with no river view)!

All of the passengers were tired, sweaty, hot and ready to get back to the ship for cool showers, cocktails, and incidentally, my Introduction to Manaus talk. But we passed the Meeting of the Waters once more, searched for dolphins and were treated on board to one of the delicacies of the area – fresh raw cashews, unsalted, and icy Antárctica beer. All was well. The Brazilian guide, after my suggestion, gave a little spiel on the "caju" in Brazil, and the fact the cashew nut we all love is just at the tip of the fruit. The Brazilians love the fruit just as much and make jelly out of it.

After everyone returned to "Adventurer," all taking showers at the same time (cold water, who cares?) and changing into "casual tropic" clothes, most gathered in the lounge for drinks and my talk. Willie wired me up, got my DVD with a few slides set up and me with a clicker to run it and away we went. I introduced myself very briefly and launched into the talk (not equivalent to the regular a.m. and p.m. talks on board, shorter). Here's the gist of it.

Manaus began as early as 1669 with a Christian mission, but not much really happened until the 19th century. Then it boomed – raw rubber collected drop by drop in small containers from arrow shaped gashes in the trunks of thousands of trees in the jungles surrounding the town brought prosperity and riches. That is, to a select few! The story of the labor to extract the latex is one of the most despicable in Brazil's history, and that's saying something. Natives and poor migrants from Brazil's Northeast paid the price. Electricity was developed in Manaus and plants for local rubber processing, so all would not have to be shipped to Belém one thousand miles down river to be processed. The port of Manaus was greatly improved in the 1890s to handle shipping with the big innovation being the pontoon system for the floating docks – a necessity to deal with the 70-foot variation of Rio Negro depth from wet to dry seasons. The boom lasted until 1920, lessened when rubber tree seeds were smuggled out of the country by an Englishman and transplanted in the far East, Malaysia and Sri Lanka mainly.

World War II and Hitler's submarines cut off the Asian supply so there was a very brief "renaissance" from 1942 to 1945. That ended with the war's end and the rapid development of artificial rubber for the tires of the American auto industry. An important part of my own research was SEMTA the government effort to send poor northeasterners from the drought region to Amazonia to work on the plantations, a grizzly story in itself. The workers fared almost as badly as the indigenous peoples did decades earlier. See the map for a general view. Henry Ford had tried his own rubber venture with Fordlandia in Pará State in 1928, almost two hundred miles south of Santarém (five hundred miles east of Manaus) on the banks of the Tapajós River, a major tributary of the Amazon. But that flopped by 1934, mainly due to rubber tree blight from planting the trees too close together (as opposed to open space in the original forest). That and the fact the strictly "North American" regime of non-Brazilian food, no alcohol, and the epitome of the "company store" was a hard row to hoe for the Brazilian workers. Manaus itself declined greatly until 1967 and the Free Zone. Incredible growth came since along with manufacturing of all things, computers and electronics! And tourism!

There is an entire complicated history to all this – first the decimation of the local Indian population of hunters-gatherers used to collect the rubber. It amounted to slavery and decimated the population. But the barons grew rich and enjoyed an opulent life style. The best example will be the Opera House we shall see tomorrow. The Northeasterners came in 1942 via the SEMTA program, and incidentally with them, the folk poets who would tell their story (this gave me two minutes to tell them of my research specialty, Northeastern Brazilian folklore, folk poetry and literature and a promise for much more to come with the on board talks.)

But just as important, Manaus became the hub of commercial activity in a huge area in the central amazon with Amazonas the largest Brazilian State. Fishing, jute production, cattle ranches and dairies along the feeder streams, and commerce and stores for the river dwellers arriving via a fleet of small and medium sized passenger boats to the port. Many of the "barcos" came from up to 100 miles away, Manaus being the main market for foodstuffs and the small things you need in life. After the big dock was built ocean freighters arrived to take the products to the rest of Brazil, just one example those terrific cashew nuts we enjoyed today. And Guaraná soft drinks. So, the huge fruit and vegetable market at the side of the river, the famous pavilion and fish market above, the busy downtown stores and mainly the Opera House are on tap for tomorrow morning and afternoon. (You will want to break for lunch on the "Adventurer" and a cool shower before the p.m. outing to the Opera House.) And a personal guarantee – the best coconut ice cream you will ever taste and enjoy, a personal stop before and after our Opera House tour. Dress tropical "cool". Tomorrow morning, we will be in the middle of the fruit and vegetable market with huge piles of bananas and pineapples. You might wear gloves and watch out for anything that moves! Buck and Kelly will be right beside you.

I'm leaving the Opera House in all its glory so it will be a surprise but a local guide and myself will be on hand to explain as we go along. Just the folklore: almost everything was imported from Europe for construction ending in 1896, including the many tapestries, beautiful marble from Italy, but the floors are of the most beautiful Brazilian hardwoods available (we'll put on fuzzy slippers to slide around). Opera singers from Europe came for a one-night stand, including Caruso! Now that's folklore! And the rubber barons supposedly sent their weekly laundry to Europe. Me, I'm wondering about the lack of air conditioning, the formal concert attire. You can check it all out. An unforgettable experience is ahead!

6

DAY TWO IN MANAUS – COCONUT ICE CREAM AND ...

July 3rd. The next day we were all off at 8:00 a.m. to downtown and the sights. It was a hot but short walk from the "Adventurer," past that dock entry box and a block or two to the "peoples'" dock and market. A guard said so many people could not safely navigate the area and called a buddy who actually herded us all up the steps of the "sea wall" to the overlook of the docks and river. That was probably for the best. You could see clearly the massive amount of activity of sweaty men unloading everything from cases of beer bottles to watermelons to coconuts (they tossed them one by one) to shore from local ferries and cargo boats. Women with packages and bundles on their heads passed by in a steady line weaving their way through the morass of piles of vegetables and plank walkways from the boats, all heading I surmise to the big markets up on top. There were dozens of passenger and cargo boats, rounded in front and with hammocks strung on the passageways and interior. These were the "taxis" of the Amazon Basin. Oh yeah, and there were the "garbagemen of Brazil," the ubiquitous vultures ["urubus"] everywhere, daring to come close to the vittles on the shore.

The view from up above was stunning and all the passengers were busy with their cameras (I warned of thieves but to no avail). The river level was in fact about half-way to high (or low) level, some 30 feet from the bottom of the 70-foot wall, so the boats and market were plenty close enough for filming. The Rio Negro was on the other side, busy with all manner of traffic. **This** was the image thought of by many before and after visiting Manaus. But there was much more to come.

Outline, Manaus Market, Early Morning

The Adolfo Lisboa Market is yet a highlight of Manaus, but there is pro and con. Done in 1882 and patterned on Les Halles Market in Paris, the main outdoor market is made of steel and all imported from France. Next door is the mason constructed building of the same period. What's a good market like? Smelly. Hot. Grubby in spots. The market today is all this because of the food stalls featuring fish of the region, fresh meat, other edibles. Our passengers were most interested in the fish market but were disappointed (not quite as Willie advertised). There were many varieties of fresh fish, but smaller and fewer types. The fishmongers all complain and say you should have seen it fifty years ago, then it was something! You can see a mounted Pirarucu hanging from the ceiling, the largest species of fish in Amazon waters at up to 7 or 8 feet and close to 200 lbs. But no fresh ones were seen. They say they are fish farming them but the real ones are in danger of vanishing and hard to come by. What you do see are piles of Peacock Bass, a fine tasting fish sought after for many. And the larger Tambaqui. There are probably twenty other types I can't remember, but it was a treat to see the fishmongers sharpen and handle their razor-edge knifes to dress products for the public. There is the meat market as well and you better have a strong constitution to see all the cuts hanging from stalls. And as I mentioned, incidentally there are many food stands outside the market where you can get a simple meal of rice, local vegetables and choose between many types of grilled fish.

The other part of the market is dedicated to regional handicrafts, herbal remedies (including a local Viagra substitute), "snake oil" as it were, and what we used to call in Brazil "bugigangas" or "gadgets" or "stuff." I suppose if you really took your time you might find something of interest, I thought it was junky. Oh, you could get a key chain with a piranha head on it. Blue Morphos encased in glass. (Don't allow yourself to think about this.) Lots of bows and arrows, Indigenous head dresses, how much actually made by native peoples or even others in Brazil I don't know but I doubt. Adventurers looked dutifully and later informed me they agreed with my take. They admired the steel structure itself and the fact it all came by ship up the Amazon. We repaired to the ship for cool showers, a light lunch and were off at 2:00 to the real highlight, the "Teatro Amazonas" or Opera House.

IA arranged for vans to take folks to the Opera House or "Teatro Amazonas," but leaving 30 minutes after the passengers who chose to walk through the downtown commerce and on up the slight hill to the edifice. We would all meet outside at 2:30 at the Ice Cream Shop to its side. I of course and a local security man hired by IA accompanied the groups that wanted to see the stores, some I guess wanting to shop some, but hey you can't carry a 32-inch color TV in your luggage! What they mainly were exposed to was the intensity of the commerce, the blaring noise from competing p.a. systems with shouts ("pregões") of "ofertas" and

Forró music. And pretty local girls in low cut blouses urging passersby to come on in and look around! Small and large appliances, stereos, TVs, watches (want a Rolex?) and, ahem, junk. The stores were supposedly air conditioned but open to the street, so at least you felt some blowing air. By the way you want ceiling ventilator fans in the tropics and not electric air conditioning (unless you are rich and know the repair man); the humid climate rusts out a window unit in a year's time.

Opera House Exterior

The "Teatro Amazonas" or "Opera House" is a spectacle even from a distance, the brilliant shiny mosaic domed roof with some 36,000 pieces of decorated ceramic tiles in the colors of the Brazilian flag, its pink exterior color, and the Brazilian mosaic sidewalks surrounding it and at its entrance. We all did make the ice cream stop and that evening I was told by some it was the best stop in the two days in Manaus. Coconut ice cream you could die for, even if you don't like coconut, huge scoops in cups with those tiny spoons. The essence of flavor and coldness, giving you a headache if you eat too fast. As promised, after the tour many went for seconds, me among them! Brazilian currency was in short supply but the owners were happy to accept dollar bills.

The Amazon Legend, the Opera House

The Opera House took years to build, the idea that the richness of the boom era deserved a place to show off the wealth, maybe a "wannabe" place to be like Milan. It was inaugurated in1896 with "La Gioconda" sung by Enrico Caruso. Its highlights were the steel exterior walls from Glasgow, marble from Carrara, beautiful interior paintings by the best of European artists of the times, the huge curtain of "The Meeting of the Waters" (with luscious nymphs frolicking alongside mythic river creatures) created and painted in Europe. And 198 chandeliers of Murano Glass! Statues and busts of famous creators of opera including Carlos Gomes a Brazilian! (The most famous opera in Brazil is his "O Guarani" based on a romantic novel by José de Alencar with an indigenous Romeo and Juliet!) There are also busts of the most famous writers of Brazilian literature, Machado de Assis the most celebrated. Caned seats throughout. Decorated private boxes on three upper floors. But just as impressive, the Brazilian contribution: polished, gorgeous Brazilian hardwood floors throughout (I mention the required fuzzy slippers to not damage it). No one could tell me (or us) the name of all the woods, but definitely Brazilian rosewood; but colors are light and dark. The story of Brazilian hardwoods is sad and I'll mention it in a talk on the ship. Also sad is the lugubrious story of native semi-slave labor used to build the Opera House, not a happy chapter in Brazilian History.

That and the ice cream finished the day. Everyone refreshed with yet another cool shower and a change to casual on-ship attire headed to the cocktail hour. People already knew each other a bit better, including me knowing the staff and some of them. Conversation then and at dinner was indeed lively, each person with a favorite memory and perhaps a critique or two or three of the two intense days. Dinner was filet of Tambaqui, Peacock Bass or Pirarucu (I don't know where they found that but Hotel Manager Gino Amato has his magic ways) fresh from the market, fresh vegetables, rice, and, what else, gallons of that coconut ice cream Gino saw fit to carry and somehow keep cold to the ship. I was complimented on both my preparation and presence on the excursions. Willie said the truth was I didn't know one fish from another. Not true - I had seen a real Pirarucu landed and thrown into the hold of the Milk Boat in Manaus years earlier and Piranha and Surubim on the São Francisco. He's right about all the others, maybe 100 of them.

Belém is 1000 miles downriver toward the Atlantic. "Adventurer's" top speed is 20 knots, 23 mph, so the Captain calculates 2 ½ days of travel. The "Adventurer" will have both big diesel engines at full bore for the next two days and one half to get us into Belém. The truth was and is you feel like you are in the middle of a very large lake or even the ocean as you travel the Amazon, and the small villages we basically had already experienced were often on the distant shore. I'm on to "on board" routine next.

7

ON BOARD TO BELÉM – THE "ADVENTURER" EXPERIENCE

July 4th. There's no way I can sugar coat it, the one thousand miles could be monotonous. We would be passing a fairly major city, Santarém, the next night; that was the problem, not much to see then. It was on the Tapajós River, a major tributary to the Amazon and of fame of Fordlandia two hundred miles downstream (south). Tiny villages along the river would get excited when we passed, many small canoes and boats racing to come along side, but Captain Tony had told everyone to look and not attempt to touch! Any further jungle experience would take place in Belém where in fact the flora and fauna offered more than Manaus. "Adventurer" would be doing flat out 20 knots so that would put us in Belém at midnight tomorrow night.

It was time to shine for IA staff and they and did! First things first – food! Early risers could go to the Chart Room for a big mug of coffee, then down a deck to the coffee bar outside the dining room for what was a delicious "starter" – café latte or cappuccino, pineapple, orange slices, juice, croissants and if you wanted, slices of Pound or Chocolate cake. Many went up to the fitness center (I wondered, before or after the chocolate cake?) where there were stretching exercises and yoga available. At 7:00 a.m. sharp the dining room opened with a complete, tasty buffet breakfast. It was that first morning when I noticed most of the staff eating together outside the entrance to the dining room at tables and booths to one side of the corridor. Sure enough, there was Amy and she waved me over with a big smile. We had about twenty minutes of private conversation before others arrived to join the group.

We swapped stories about graduate school, she at Cornell, me at Georgetown, but much more about shared experiences in Brazil. She had read "Adventures of a 'Gringo' Researcher" so she knew a lot more about me than I her, and said she has some questions for me about all that. I asked if she was tempted by a double major, adding Ornithology to the Hotel Management. "No, but I can get dates from the birders by just mentioning my degree from Cornell! Chuckle." Preliminaries out of the way: I told Amy a bit about Molly, how it was all "tabled" as it were, but that I had some previous girl friends in Rio. For her part she said right now traveling the world with a terrific company like AT and being on the "Adventurer" were enough for her. And like me there were friends left in Brazil but nothing going on right now. She was not ready to be a homemaker and Mom, sometime but not yet. But she added, and it made me blush, "I haven't met anyone quite like you yet. Miguel, I think we are going to be good friends. We can't be running around together on board but there's always unexpected quiet time before bedtime. I have to get away from the constant demands, complaints and all. My room number is 504, down the hall from Steve Barber's, but he is a "cool dude" and understands that I've got to have another life than that damned desk in Staff Quarters. Consider this an official 'invite' for a drink and talk to get to know each other better." I gave her my room number as well, just in case!

There was time to say hello to Steve, and some of the staff. Birders were already out on the observation deck but Steve outlined the day, the talks and other duties. Kelly, Willie and Eli were at the next table and said hello, and asked how was I doing. "So far so good." I was assured I had not seen anything yet! Then it was off to the dining room to meet adventurers and have breakfast.

Orange juice, great "café com leite," pineapple, scrambled eggs and too much bacon, wonderful bread from the ship bakery, and yes, a slice of chocolate cake got me off to a more than needed start of the day. No one is particularly awake or really wanting to socialize at that hour, so there was just a bit of chit-chat with adventurers from Jacksonville, Florida was it. I do recall they run a chain of bookstores in the South and we agreed to talk about southern writers later. They looked up my writings once they had seen the trip brochure and said all would be on the shelves by the time we got back. Hurrah.

It was fitting that AL Steve would give the first talk at 9:00 a.m. A long – time veteran of AT trips all over the world, his original expertise was oceanography, seas and waters of the world. He outlined the North and South Atlantic oceans and how the Amazon fit into the scheme of things, gave all the statistics about the river, length, volume of water discharged into the Atlantic, largest in the world and more than the next seven rivers. Width at its mouth, depending how you measure it, 10 miles the main current, but up to 110 with tributaries from the neighboring Pará river from Belém and more. And with Buck Weylander's help, the animals and fish thriving in the river, some of which we had seen in Manaus. All came illustrated with wonderful images on the high definition screens in the lounge. (And a few surprises at cocktail hour)

After a break I was scheduled for my first talk (not counting that introduction to Manaus). This is what they were paying me for! I did not use images the first talk but relied on language, facts, jokes and all I had learned over many years of what makes Brazil tick. The talk was one hour and I got through all the outline below:

An Introduction to Brazil

I. The Brazilians and a Glance into the Brazilian Character

    a. "El español es lindo; o português é bacana."

    b. "A loura suada" [the sweaty blonde]. "Sem bigode" [no mustache]. "Sem colarinho" [no collar please]. All terms for "Choppe" draft beer. Good brewmeisters (all Nazi refugees goes the natl. joke).

    c. Land of the future; always was; always will be (and is in 1972).

    d. Revolution of 1964 – Tanks on Avenida Atlântica in Rio; traffic jam on beach; a bit of a bother.

    e. "O jeito." "Somos comodistas, não comunistas." Avoid bloodshed; but lack of violence a national stereotype; it has all changed.

    f. "Apareça." Come on by and see me sometime.

    g. "Buttons" The question of physical distance during conversation.

    h. Snapshot: painting the national library.

    i. Snapshot: adjusting the mirror

    j. "Peba. Peba." ["Armadillo. Armadillo"]

II. Brazil: An Introduction

    a. Size/ population/ "they speak Portuguese"/

    b. The Brazilian mosaic – Portuguese, African, German, Italian, Native Indian, Japanese, and yes from American Civil War

    c. The land: desert/ rich farm land/ plantation economy/ savannah/ jungle

    d. National hyperbole: language most difficult/ best looking women/ richest resources / industrialization, globalization n. 1 in world several products,

    e. Swim attire: maiô/ biquini/ tanga/ fio dental [dental floss]

    f. Religion: Catholic, Nominal Catholic, African Religion (xangô, candomblé), Umbanda, Kardec Spiritist, Protestant, Mormon

g. Carnaval, Land of!
h. Today's problems: rich-poor/ drugs/ violence, hunger but there is good news: oil, lots of land and good land, hardworking people.
i. History: Blame it on Portugal (Portuguese jokes)
j. Flexible Character, mixture of race White, black, and all others (160 categories once upon a time)

It went phenomenally well with lots of laughter and applause. An Aside. All seemed amazed at Gaherty's facility in Portuguese ("That's funny. You don't look Brazilian!") There was one critique by one person: my first talk was not up-to-date. "Explain this more." My defense: it was not supposed to be "up to date" but an historic introduction.

8

THE NATURALISTS' WORLD

The p.m. was dedicated to the naturalists and it was great, and with a surprise or two. There was plenty of time and each would get his or her turn. Jack Bataldi started things off with "Birds of the Amazon," a bewildering variety of macaws, parrots, songbirds, seabirds migrated upstream, toucans and yes four varieties of vultures. (I can't help but interject – there is a great story-poem from Brazil's folk-popular literature where a vulture is the main character, but he's a **Catholic** vulture who defends the faith against one of those pesky Protestant missionaries.) I don't know where he got all the images; they looked out of the pages of "National Geographic" or "Audubon" to me. We did not see that many on the outing from Manaus; Jack patiently explained that the adage is true – "The early bird gets the worm" - and early risers see the birds. A little while after dawn they all hunker down in that immense underbrush and high trees; a good Ornithologist can tell you who's there by their sound or call. (A few phony birdcalls came from the audience and much laughter.) A great talk and just one of many to come; Jack would really get it on when "Adventurer" reached ocean waters.

The second was by Kelly teamed with Buck the last one-half hour. Kelly showed us a dazzling array of images of butterflies, including those Blue Morphos we saw on the canoe trip (Did I mention they were in the big market, in glass boxes as tourist souvenirs? If every tourist takes just one home, well, figure it out yourself.) She than had amazing images of Amazon leaf cutter ants. She said if you want a little fun see Charlton Heston's old movie from 1954, "The Naked Jungle" based on "Leiningen and the Ants," a sixteen-page short story. It deals with a huge swath of army ants migrating and headed to Heston's cocoa plantation in the Amazon. It is an epic battle and it scared the devil out of me years ago. Of course, I was only 13. She then opened a box on the podium, turned it over and a huge tarantula slowly crawled out. After a few people shrieked and the ones in the front row jumped up and retreated back toward the wall, Kelly said, "These guys have a bad reputation but in reality, they are very gentle." To prove her point she picked it up, but somehow the damned thing slipped out of her hand, hit the floor at a fast run and was down the aisle to the door leading to the passenger rooms. She laughed, bounded out the same door and corralled it halfway down the corridor. With may I say, a shit-eating grin, she continued the talk, explaining how they love those bananas and plantains we saw in the market yesterday, but "Jo Jo" (it was a girl) would be locked up for now and released at Belém in the zoo, supposedly to check out their bananas. Much applause and guffaws followed her exit.

Then Buck came in with a long pole and this furry critter hanging from it – an Amazon Sloth. "Never fear folks, this guy doesn't move as fast as Kelly's friend. Let me tell you all about him and some of his friends in the forest." What followed was an illuminating, at least for me, account of this gentle, shy animal Buck had "borrowed for a few days" from the zoo in Manaus (with the proviso he turns it in at the Belém zoo tomorrow or the next day). He said, "Shy the Sloth will live on a tether on a place set up just for him on the back deck. If you'd like to get to know him come on out during cocktail hour. He sleeps a lot and likes to be in bed by dark, so check the time. I'll throw a light blanket over his branch for the night." We learned all about sloths, different species of Amazon monkeys including the famous endangered Golden Lion Tamarin (Buck said we would be able to see one in the zoo in Belém and perhaps a wild one in the Atlantic Rain Forest along the east coast of Brazil). In a way it was a bit depressing as Buck showed image after image, many of the animals in danger of extinction. But he closed with an upbeat statement on how there is a vibrant ecological movement and community that is doing miracles in preservation work.

Everyone was ready for a return to "civilization" and the bar with those p.m. cocktails, but conversation buzzed about what a great first day aboard! Someone said, "AT has a reputation for all this, but I'm not sure I can take any more show and tell right now." A bespectacled gentleman and his cheery wife asked me to join them for a drink, "Maybe more of that McCallans I saw you drink last night." Hmm. Apparently, one is not always aware they are being watched. He said it in a good-natured way, adding I had good taste and he would join me. Their question: are Brazilians **really** the way I described them in the talk that a.m.? I laughed and said only: "This is what many years of study of Portuguese Language and Brazilian Culture and many trips to Brazil have revealed to me. There's no exaggeration. Times will change and I'm sure some of this will too, but I think that reveals why I love Brazil so much." They turned out to be Robert and Claire Callahan from Kearney, Nebraska, veterans of AT travel and out to see more of the world. We would have long talks about farming in Nebraska. He had farmed two thousand acres of corn, wheat and alfalfa and both were graduates of U. of Nebraska. We talked about tractors. Oh yeah, and Big Red Football.

Tonight was our first really settled in dinner on board, and it was that ship experience, the "Captain's Dinner." I have no experience in this travel and sea world, but understand it is a custom on many ships. Back home we would say "Putting on the dog!" It meant more than casual, a sport coat, shirt and tie if you have it, and nice dresses for the ladies, and the Captain and his staff in dress whites! The Portuguese know how to do this! Captain Antônio introduced perhaps six of his main crew during the cocktail hour, Second in Command on the Bridge, Martin Mendes the Executive Officer (the jack of all trades assigned to iron out any on ship difficulties), of course Gino Amato and Joana Oliveira once again. And our chef, who else? Reynaldo Romano from Roma (a happy coincidence, lots of stories of relatives who cooked in the Vatican) who took a bow in his chef's hat and apron and promised us a wonderful dinner. And not to forget a large, ruddy faced man – João Tavares Chief Engineer who would keep us running. "Denizen of the depths" they called him, spending most of his time in the bowels of the ship.

There is an entire cadre of other people – the Thai staff, men and women, who served at table, did room maintenance and the super-efficient laundry room. The guys doubled on zodiac duty, life boat activity, and lots of cleaning and scrubbing the decks. The ladies served in the lounge during cocktail hour as well. We would gradually meet them, many also veterans of years of service on AT trips. I got a kick out of their form of address, always calling me "Mr. Mike." It took a while to get to know them, but the maître-d, servers in the dining room and Maria the pretty young thing in charge of cleaning my room became friends. I would see later that Captain Tony insisted on a "Thai" night later at sea with they in local dress and with Thai food and dancing. A huge success.

I don't know if it matters much when you are paying up to $32,000 per person for the entire trip, but tonight was a "freebie" from IT and the Captain: champagne before dinner, assorted wines with dinner, cognac over coffee after dinner. The food tonight was not "Amazon," but rather, filet mignon, lobster tail, Caesar salad, wonderful baked, French bread, and perhaps the best dessert of the trip, a rich, chocolate, coconut cake you could die for. Oh, for a select few, special dietary plates from the kitchen, vegetables for the vegans, and basically special orders for the picky. I did notice that the large majority accepted the Captain's hospitality.

Coming in late as would be the custom from the tidying up the lounge, most tables were full but one fellow waved to me from one of the large oval tables and asked me to join his group. What a deal that turned out to be. He was some beyond middle age, probably in his late 60s, his wife a stunning dark-haired beautiful lady twenty years younger and three other couples who all seemed to know each other. The surprise was the conversation was entirely in Portuguese, Brazilian variant at that! He introduced himself his wife Uíara and the others, but I didn't really catch all the names. They were good friends and colleagues from Itamarati the Brazilian State Department, and the trip was celebrating my new friend, Leonel Peixoto's retirement after thirty years of service.

Leonel embraced me, shook my hand firmly and gave me the most memorable compliment of the trip, "Rapaz, você acertou absolutamente nesta palestra! Nem nós os Brasileiros, nos damos conta da totalidade da imagem que você apresentou. Parabens e parabens de novo!" He said they all howled at the jokes, the tidbits of Brazilian slang, and basically marveled at how I came to that knowledge. I think I was stammering by this time, overwhelmed with the intensity of the moment, but managed to say it had taken years of study, travel and research. And keeping my eyes and ear open. I mentioned my literary model was the young Luís Fernando Veríssimo and his "Chronicles" of daily life in Brazil (and his father, a diplomat serving in Washington D.C. and writing "Gato Preto em Campo de Neve" ["Black Cat in a Field of White"].) Leonel slapped his forehead saying "I don't believe it. Jóia, rapaz" ["Wonderful, young man"]. And I had the best of Brazilian mentors (I mentioned three or four); he knew them all and some on a first name basis.

In Brazil, he explained, the primary requisite for high diplomatic service was a broad knowledge of your country and especially your language and culture (although he admitted family connections could and did at times play a role). Over that first glass of champagne I mentioned that I had the pleasure of knowing Adriano da Gama Kury, the top flight preparer of Brazilians to take the Itamarati Portuguese Exam, the first and major hurdle to be accepted to diplomatic service. He almost yelled, "Adriano was my mentor years ago. Que mundo pequeno! I thought I knew it all before I went to his private classes and he straightened me out quick!" I said, "I've got to ask? Do you know Vinicius de Morais?" [Brazil's most famous unorthodox diplomat, one of its best poets, and known to like his

Scotch]. He laughed loudly and said, "I can't count the times I've been drunk under the table by that fellow. He breaks all the rules but has been truly one of our best ambassadors to the world. And, hey, he's not a bad poet. (Understatement intentional)." I said, "Meus Deus but do we have a lot to talk about; my job is to mix with all the adventurers but hopefully we'll have many times together. He nodded in agreement and tackled the steak and lobster."

So the time passed quickly, too quickly but all too pleasantly. I mainly listened to Leonel and his friends' tales of diplomatic service all over the globe, caught tidbits of their wives' world and just enjoyed the moment. Who could have imagined such people on board? Leonel explained that he and his friends had traveled the world and much of Brazil but this trip was ideal even for them to experience a whirlwind overview of their country. He added, "When's your next talk? We don't want to miss that." I said probably after Belém and on down the coast to Fortaleza, but that they would be sick of hearing me by the time we got to Porto Alegre!

On the way out I passed by a table where Amy was sitting with Steve and some of the adventurers. She said, "Can you call me in an hour?" "Fine, will do." After the call and "Come up and see me some time! Ha ha" I knocked on her cabin door up on Bridge Deck about 9:00 p.m., just down the way from AL Leader Steve's. She and Steve were very good friends (I haven't mentioned, never romantically involved, he married and a faithful husband at that, she on her own), but with great work chemistry over many trips for AT. He respected her much needed moments of privacy, this being one of them.

Her cabin was as expected quite a bit different from mine, for openers, a divan and easy chair, and a sliding glass door out to a small balcony, and a big desk. It was highly organized but with professional clutter – two different telephones (one ship, one land), stacks of manilla folders each with a single date, the plan for that day on the trip. I noticed two photos, one a family picture with I surmise her parents, sister and two brothers and her a teenager, the other with a shot of her in Rockefeller Center with a young man, both in winter attire.

Still in an attractive blue outfit from the Captain's dinner, she opened the door and surprised me by planting a warm kiss on my lips, gratefully returned, saying "That's how I say hello to special friends. Hope I don't offend you. Come on in, I've got a nice bottle of Drambuie and there's time for an after-dinner sip or two." I sat in one of easy chairs and she on the divan and we had a great talk. You know when someone is easy to get along with, and it's mutual? Well, that was the case. Conversation came easily and we covered a lot of ground.

Amy was from Denver, her father a lawyer with his own small practice downtown, her mother a registered nurse still working at Denver's main downtown hospital, this after raising the four children. It was a Catholic family, Irish but not "crazy" Irish, and Amy admitted that AT work did not facilitate much church going; we could talk more about that some time. After undergraduate work at C.U. in Boulder in Business Management and a minor in Spanish, she had garnered a full ride for the Hotel Management program at Cornell. While there she continued to work on Spanish and did an intensive course in Brazilian Portuguese, looking to be a manager for Marriott or the like in one of the big cities in Latin America. After two years with Marriott in Buenos Aires, she learned about the Getúlio Vargas Foundation in Rio and its' Brazilian Business program, made the big decision to go back to school and spent an entire year in Rio. That's when AT learned of her and offered the AAL job just two years ago. I was trying to do all the math in my head and had figured her to be about 28, not far off as it turned out, 29 later this year. In the two years she had logged no less than 20 trips, and said she thinks she has pretty much "seen it all."

Amy had read my "Adventures" but not "Letters" (maybe a good thing with all the liaisons with the Brazilian women). I told her about my friendship with Chico Buarque and the "Arretado" ["Cool Guy"] nickname and "Mistakes of Our Youth" business, asking would it be possible to get him on board for a night or two. She said she would immediately get e-book versions of "Letters" and read all about it. (I said there were some amorous moments in that series that might tell her more than she needed to know about me, but the story with Chico was more important.) She said, "Wow! I am a major fan, but being on the ships did not hear anything about this." Amy doubted my idea for no better reason than his price tag but said she, I and Eli could put our heads together and talk about it. Like me she thought the sophisticated, highly poetic and double entendre language of his songs would be far beyond adventurers' appreciation. I thought maybe we could do the Rock n' Roll and he just his most famous "easy" sambas. She heard my talk yesterday (sitting in the back row of the lounge, on call as it were) and said she loved it and by the audience response said I'm assured to being off to a great start on IA. We talked of plans for Belém, some still in the works, but said she would "connect" tomorrow night for a quick hello at cocktails, otherwise busy, except for now. She asked me to join her on the divan, we drank one more noggin of liqueur and we kissed again, this time initiated by me and not rejected. I think I might even have accidentally touched her breasts and caused a quickening of pulse on both our parts, but she pulled away, laughing with those sparkling blue eyes, and said, "Mike it's going to be a long trip. We'll get to it later." We both agreed that what we needed to talk more about was mutual experience and love of Brazil, but no time tonight.

I slipped out her door on 5th level, walked on clouds down to third and was soon sawing logs before a very busy and entertaining day. Santarém to Belém arrival estimated for midnight.

9

⸻⸻◆⸻⸻

DAY TWO ON THE AMAZON – SANTARÉM TO BELÉM "AT SEA" WISDOM AND SHENANIGANS

July 5th. The next morning outside the dining room Steve sidled up, a mischievous and knowing look in his eye and said I would not have to do a regular time slot talk on Belém; he would appreciate perhaps twenty minutes of general highlights or if I needed 30 at CC. He would handle nuts and bolts for the two days ashore with all options (the adventurers would sign up tonight for their interests). He said all of us could chip in tomorrow night for thoughts about the day and the next to come. Today he would give adventurers a bit more leisure time, scheduling just two talks. He added that he would like my second talk on Brazil for the day at sea following Belém.

I made sure to say hello to staff people and chat a bit, noticing that Amy was not present, must be down in the staff office setting up shore stuff for Belém. Willie was in a bit of a dither saying he needed some extra time to get ready for the p.m. talk, something about lots of diving at Manaus. I had yet to have a real conversation with Harry Downing but hoped to soon; he was due for first talk today. After just a few minutes I moved on into the dining room, still fairly empty with lots of empty tables. I am finding that no one is quite awake at that hour and many do not wish to be disturbed,

55

so I sat at one of the empty tables. One of the solo adventurers, a fellow from Vancouver it turns out, did sit down. He once again was a long-time veteran of AT trips, had served in the Canadian Air Force at CFB Comox Air Base on Vancouver Island. One of my loves has always been flying and planes and I could name WWII and Korea U.S. fighters but honestly was ignorant of the Canadian planes, wondering if they would be the same as the British, i.e. the famous Spitfire. He filled me in with more detail than I needed to know.

Next was an experience – Harry Downing's talk on the European competition to obtain riches in the New World, some legitimate discovery and exploration, some downright skullduggery and even piracy. I discovered along with the few new adventurers why Harry Downing is one of the longest serving full-time employees of AT and pardon the term "a crowd favorite." British, old school, with ties to Oxford and an undergraduate degree in Theology, preparing like many upper-class Brits for a career in the Church (Anglican that is), Harry was way-laid by early teenage travels throughout Europe "with a knapsack on his back." AT discovered him now at Cambridge "for meals" as he put it, doing graduate work in World History, albeit with a British slant.

Harry made no secret of the enmity between Spain and Portugal and his own England, culminating in Queen Elizabeth's order to Sir Francis Drake and others to "singe the beard of Phillip II of Spain," beginning a tradition of legalized piracy (the Buccaneers) to attack, pillage and plunder any ports known to have Spanish gold and silver and to even attack the Spanish Treasure Fleet (the Galleons) on the high seas. "El Draque" was the worst or the best, depending on your point of view, successfully attacking Vera Cruz in Mexico, Cartagena de Indias in Colombia, Santiago in Chile, Lima in Peru, Acapulco in Mexico and even San Francisco on the outposts of Spanish Influence. Harry told the entire story, Portugal and Brazil not entering so much mainly because gold and diamonds were not discovered in Brazil until the 18th century.

And there was veiled to be sure criticism of Rome and the Popes, the Spanish Inquisition and the "Patronato Real" Spain's official policy of combining church and State, the king naming the hierarchy of the Church, and the Church subservient to the Crown. (I have to confess I don't see much difference between that and King Henry VIII's rule.) Although I had studied all this from the Peninsular point of view, the grandeur of the voyages of discovery and conquest, I was aware of both sides of the question, particularly the violence, enslavement of the Indigenous population of the New World harnessed as manual labor for the haciendas and mines.

For sure England was not lily-white, consider the slave trade to its colonies in North America and squashing any opposition. But that's a topic for another day. I noticed my diplomat friends questioning of Harry after the talk, and they were educated and knew the facts. All agreed that it was an age of greed and shame on all parts. Just an aside, not mentioned so far, the exploration and first discoveries in the Amazon Basin were in fact largely due to the legend of "El Dorado" and **all** the European nations' lust for gold.

It was Harry's beautiful King's English delivery of his material, a very sharp wit with salt and pepper moments of sarcasm, all in all a profound sense of humor that made him a favorite of all of us. Indeed, from a speaker's point of view he was a very hard act to follow. None followed that morning; we all enjoyed a nice lunch and there was a time for a nap before the afternoon highlights, and that they were!

A hard act to follow did not apply in this case. All that didn't matter when it came to Willie Walsh; he in the parlance "couldn't give a fig" whenever he came on. His talk at 2:00 p.m. was liberally accompanied by terrific film footage of his dives during the almost three days in Manaus, many of which we had no idea about. He had video VHS film of the fish market with comments on all the species we saw, the pink dolphins at the Meeting of the Waters and new to us, the lagoon and igarapé we visited afterwards. Basically, his message about the latter was "a good thing no one went for a swim. I've got some surprises for you." In that very clear water, he showed several varieties of the same fish from the market, some beautiful tropical fish living under the huge "Victoria Regina" lily pads we saw from the canoes and a small alligator resting on top of one of them. But then came the surprise – yes, piranhas, taken at a distance but unmistakable. Willie assured us that if they had been in the swimming area, roped off near the lodge, we would have been forewarned. He did proceed to scare the daylights out of us afterwards though – a video clip of a capybara crossing a stream, the sudden massive thrashing in the water, and the capybara's bones floating to the top. Willic asked if anyone bought those piranha key chains from the market? He said, "Those were the babies."

He ended the talk with a flourish, offering his own surprise added to yesterday's talks - he took a covering off a three by three cage and pulled out a six-foot boa constrictor wrapped around his arm. More screams and starts from the audience! "This is a baby as well, pretty lethargic for the moment since we've fed him two meaty agoutis (like a big guinea pig) this morning. He will grow, and they do live for up to 20 to 30 years, to about seven to ten feet and sixty pounds. However, he'll have to do that in the Belém zoo where I'll take him tomorrow morning."

Someone piped up, "Where did you get him, Willie?" He smiled, said "That's a secret, but let's say it was a good thing you did not walk down on the planks to the vegetable and fruit market yesterday morning in Manaus. He was hanging out, wrapped around one of the poles that supported the plank floor waiting for the lizards that hang out there. Folks, it's a bad crowd! If you want, you can come up for a closer look; I assure you he is so sleepy he will hardly notice." A few daring folks came up to look but not to touch. With that Willie ended the show saying, "We'll have all these critters ashore tomorrow morning and out of your hair."

CC - Cocktail Chatter. Mike introduced me for the "Introduction to Belém" and said, "Go ahead and take half an hour if you'd like." I had put some images of Belém on a DVD and Willie put them up, a balance of showing "previews" yet not enough to ruin the surprise of it all. They included my map and pictures of airplanes. Here's the talk:

Belém was founded in 1616 by the Portuguese; it is located 100 kilometers from the Atlantic on the Pará River with the huge island of Marajó between it and the actual Amazon. The city did not become a capital until the late 18th century, 150 years later, but Portugal did have to defend it against the local Tupinambá Indians, than incursions from the French, Dutch and English.

It is equally as important, really more so than Manaus, as the main city in the region and equally part of the Amazon Rain forest with the huge Guajará Bay in front of the city, the Pará and Guama Rivers, and hundreds of tributaries outside the city in the rain forest. Belém was a shipping port originally for latex, along with Manaus, and later for iron ore found in huge quantities in the southern part of the State. It is still a major shipping port to the rest of Brazil, South America and Europe, but tourism is important.

Culturally it is a regional variant of all Brazil with its own large Carnival and even larger "Festival de Nazaré" or the church festival of Nazareth, perhaps the largest religious party in Brazil, and that's saying something. It is the city of the "mangueiras" those large mango shade trees we shall see tomorrow. An aside, it is important to me as one of major places in Brazil for folk-popular poetry, the Guajarina Press of the 1930s and especially WW II days.

I told of my days in Belém in great detail in "Adventures" and a bit repeated here talking of the huge market, the Indigenous Museum and Zoo, and a jungle trip as the highlights (Steve will talk of this in a minute).

"I thought in my remaining minutes to tell you of something else. Here goes. I know you are thinking of how fast this amazing ship is making it the 1000 miles from Manaus to Belém so I thought I'd talk to you about airplane travel in the Amazon Basin, but with one proviso for you history buffs – the prop or propeller kind. They are just a bit faster than "Adventurer," but not much. I'll fill in a bit about Belém along the way.

"Just five short/ long years ago when I was a Fulbrighter doing research on Brazil's folk-popular literature I was near the end of my year's tenure in Brazil but had one more place to check out the poets and the booklets of narrative verse telling a story – the Amazon. I was living in Recife, Pernambuco on the bulge where Brazil is closest to Africa; we'll be there in just a few days and we've planned some amazing things for you to see. Problem was I had no money but wangled a few more hundred dollars from Fulbright to fly all the way to Manaus to check out the poets. Important stops on the way would be Fortaleza, São Luís de Maranhão, Belém and finally to Manaus. (See the map on our screens.)

The trip did not turn out to be anything really significant for cordelian research, but it was one more picturesque adventure in the great Brazil. We left Guararapes Airport in Recife early one morning on a Curtis 46 airplane, the military version of the DC-3, fare grade number III, the only fare available considering the modest financial resources remaining to me. The airline was the old standby Varig. The first stop was in Fortaleza where the plane was temporarily grounded, but after a certain amount of time we took off again, heading for São Luís, the capital of Maranhão State. There the old wreck stayed on the ground definitely. We had tried to take off from São Luís, warming up the engines at the end of the runway, but then received the order to taxi back to the hangar.

So we changed planes once again, now to a DC – 3 of Paraense Airlines, a small regional carrier in the North and the Amazon. With no more problems we arrived in Belém do Pará late in the afternoon. From the air it was all new to me, and I was very impressed by the dense tropical forest which could be seen immediately after takeoff from São Luís. THIS was the famous Amazon forest so dreamed about and imagined from readings in graduate school. (Remember, I saw Belém before Manaus; you are doing the opposite.) We flew at a very low altitude (the only way the old DC-3 could travel), so the result was a marvelous view of the forest. There seemed to be no cleared areas – all was forest, rivers and swamp.

At first view Belém seemed pretty with wide tree-lined avenues in the city center, but with extreme humidity and heat. A minor incident caused my plans to change from one day to three long days. In short, I was racing a little old lady for a taxi cab (I had to get to the airline office pronto to make connections), stepped off the curb into the gutter, and badly twisted an ankle. One of Belém's First Aid doctors said to stay off the ankle for three days. As you will see I didn't. Not by my own choice I would hobble around Belém seeing what I could and some of what you will see.

Trying to make the best of the situation, the next day I limped down to the docks of Belém to see the famous "Ver- O -Peso" Market. In spite of the ankle, I ended up seeing the most fascinating market that I had seen up to that point in Brazil, and you need to remember that I had already seen the most famous markets and fairs of the Northeast and the Northeastern fair in Rio, and the markets along the São Francisco River in Minas Gerais and Bahia, all in search of that same folk-popular poetry. I saw the docks of Belém with huge freighters of the high seas, also navigating the Pará River outside of Belém and then the Amazon itself, the docks boiling with activity.

So far so good. The accident with the badly, twisted ankle caused me to miss the Varig flight on that Saturday to Manaus. I tried to change plans and catch a Vaspe Airline flight on Sunday, at eleven a.m. to Manaus. The eleven o'clock flight was first announced as delayed, programmed for departure at two p.m. The same flight was announced as "delayed" until three p.m. The same flight was announced as delayed until seven p.m. The same flight was then cancelled. On Monday, the happy gringo with ticket in hand climbed aboard a Paraense flight to Manaus: a DC - 4 on the tarmac, motors warming up, and suddenly called back to the gate. A long wait. Finally we took off for the dreamed of, fabulous Manaus. And we made it.

What I've told you so far is the "outgoing" journey; there were other events on the "return." After several amazing days in Manaus, it was time to return to Recife, that was when there were more unexpected adventures of Brazilian aviation. The first flight was a D C - 3 back to Belém.

Everything is going too well! What is going on? The Paraense DC – 3 was programmed to leave for Belém do Pará at 6 a.m. We left only one hour later, that is at 7:00 a.m. That's the good news. Right after departure, on route to Belém, I noticed smoke and flames coming out of the right-hand engine. It did seem to diminish a bit as the landing gear went up. Happily, the pilot noticed too. We landed in Santarém and an interesting scene followed: they ordered all the passengers to get off (it was a small airplane) through the normal small ladder. Later, all of us wandering about on the tarmac, I happened across the pilot and asked, out of simple curiosity, what was the problem? These were his words, not distorted I think by translation (and paraphrased): "Hey dude, I don't know, I'm just the pilot. I just run the steering wheel. The mechanic will look into it." What bothered me a bit was his appearance: with no uniform or any other sign of a pilot of an on-going airline, he was dressed in "civilian" clothes, and a bit grease stained at that. He did not fill me with confidence.

A bit later we took off in the same airplane and returned to my by now beloved Belém. I finished the tourism I didn't do before including a small boat trip to six tributaries of the Pará River, a trip to the zoo and then time to head home to Recife. So once again, we lifted our wings for a flight to Fortaleza, and on the final point of take off at the end of the runway, we all heard a "tunk, tunk, tunk" and were called again to return to the terminal where there was a delay of one hour and once again we took to the air. This time successfully.

The rest was as we say back home "a cup of tea" or here "uma canja" [chicken soup]. Perhaps we all will be glad to roll into Belém tonight, get a good night's sleep and have two full days to experience this important Brazilian city. Steve is ready to tell you want to expect the next two days and Eli who has been conspicuous in his absence and silence has good news for all of us.

There was great applause after the talk and later on several guys who had military service and some who had flown in the same air jalopies cornered me, offered to buy drinks and swap stories of that great air age.

Steve's nuts and bolts for the two days.

Steve outlined the possibilities for the options for Belém: Tomorrow a.m. a. the huge Ver-O-Peso Market and walk to the Fort. b. The Goeldi Indigenous Cultural Center and Botanical Garden – Zoo (a.m. or p.m.) c. Local church sites: the original Jesuit Church, the Cathedral and the Our Lady of Nazaré national shrine (a.m. or p.m.) d. A small boat trip to the tributaries of the Pará river (very early a.m. either day). All would return to the ship each day for lunch (and a cold shower). Eli jumped in and added there was be regional music on the back deck tonight – local "caboclo" or Amazon "country" music.

Amy showed up for dinner and we both sat at the Brazilian diplomats' table; I thought they would really appreciate her background at Getúlio Vargas and her great Portuguese. We all toasted each other with wine from Rio Grande do Sul and dinner passed quickly. Amy said she was really under the gun to finish up the details for tomorrow's excursions plus dealing with Brazilian bureaucracy for some new and unexpected "dock fees." She said let's make a date for the night leaving Belém for the sea; no pressure for a couple of days. I quickly agreed.

So it was early to bed anticipating two huge days in the Brazilian Amazon at Belém do Pará.

10

ADVENTURING IN BELÉM

July 6th. It was a very early call, 5:30 a.m. breakfast and personal at 6:00 and out at 7:00. It was worked out so all adventurers could do all the excursions, either the Market or the Boat Ride one a.m. then the other; Churches, Teatro da Paz and Basílica de Nazaré or Goeldi Museum and Zoo in the p.m. And one could do all or none. In my case it was all and Steve had me as one of the leaders for the Ver-O-Peso Market in the a.m.

Ver – O – Peso Market

My group was twenty-five, an okay number and all hanging together. There was a local guide with questionable English (I translated a large part of it, but only after his permission; we ended friends). The market's name Ver − O - Peso is interesting coming from colonial days when the Portuguese tax collectors were stationed here and taxed all goods coming in from the jungle by checking their weight. Locals had a better version: check the weight to be sure you aren't cheated! I had major moments in the same Market in 1967 and now five years later there were lots of changes, but mainly superficial. Instead of the old canvas market stalls there were now plastic roofed sections, this on the outside. They housed mainly chickens, birds, vegetables and tourist "bugigangas" − "stuff." The inside was far more interesting, the main fish market, meat market and all the local "remedies."

Incidentally, the Ver − O - Peso is as historic as the Manaus market but much larger. It seemed a whole lot more antiseptic, but the original steel frame building is intact and beautiful with its four spires. There was a lot more shrimp but still the fresh "catch" of the day; we were told you had to be there at 4:30 a.m. for the best choice! Fish: Dourado, Filhote, and yes, several Pirarucu. And dozens of others I can't possibly translate from Portuguese. The adventurers who came along did not regret their decision. Stall after stall of men cutting up fish. Huge amounts of noise and all of us not understanding much of the chatter.

Outside what was just as interesting was the scene facing the fish market entrance; dozens of small fishing boats unloading an incredible variety of fish and vegetables and fruit, and one thing unchanged from 1967, people working in their bare feet handling 300 lb. cakes of ice, splitting it and putting it into the holds of boats ready to head out to the lakes and rivers anew. And while I think of it, there were several "cordel" poets and salesmen then, all with fascinating stories. We saw no poetry stands today and I honestly did not have time to search any out. And one more thing − in 1967 the outside market was dominated by ethnic Japanese − Brazilians, mainly with vegetables. We were told they all had moved to the south to Tomé - Açu and the interior for harvesting fruit and preparing the fruit drinks and berries to be "exported" to all of Brazil. Oh yeah, the main plaza on the other side of the fishing boats and dock was still filled with old "friends" of 1967 – dozens of black vultures ("the garbage men of Brazil") perhaps relatives or descendants of those I took pictures of then.

New were all the stands selling "açaí" fruit drinks, smoothies and a myriad of other fruit drinks. (Missing was the great coconut ice cream shop from Manaus lamented by all). In Belém there were dozens of stands with local remedies in clear plastic bottles for everything from ulcers to stomach upset, constipation, its opposite, high blood pressure and of course **ED**, erectile disfunction – all the "homemade" local Viagra remedies called "Viagra Natural."

In retrospect, I think the charm of Manaus is linked to the fact it is indeed one thousand miles upstream, on the banks of the Rio Negro and then the Solimões, and the whole rubber boom. But in reality Belém is much larger, just as historic and with local churches, Theater and Basilica more than matching Manaus, and an even larger "riverine" civilization with its huge main river the Pará heading to the ocean and the Amazon and the Guamá and other seemingly unending rivers, streams, igarapés and settlements within ten miles of Belém.

And yes, a happy coincidence, Harry was in my group and he and I had great conversation as we walked from the market, past the fishing boats, across the broad plaza and through the manicured lawns of the old Fort of Belém. He was all eyes and ears for the experience, new to him and one of the few major places on the planet he had not seen, the entire Brazil experience new except Bahia and Rio later on. He said, "I signed on to this trip exactly for that, to fill in gaps, but also a bit of a paid vacation and rest from academia (he still lectures at Oxford, part-time when home, a teaching fellow in Britain's history).

There was a compliment, Harry saying, "Mike we are on your turf and you indeed are the master storyteller here; I'm happy to absorb a little of it and will be sure and add it to the brain mass! You are doing a terrific job and the pleasure is truly mine!" I in return assured Harry that his role as historian and "keeper of the keys" of the ship library and all the talks to come would have me in the front row!

The fort itself dated back to 1616 when one of Brazil's top generals from the then successful and major Capitania (Brazil's version of "colonies") of Bahia was sent to check the incursion of the British, French and Dutch into the territory previously discovered by Portugal. The old wooden fort he established was later converted to the standard stone and mortar with battlements and cannon, and that was what we saw today. In my opinion the fort was interesting but not impressive, especially once one has seen the Spanish fort system in Cartagena, Vera Cruz or San Juan. Its own battlements and cannon faced the bay. And the view was terrific! It looked down on the commercial square in front of the Ver – O - Peso and commanded a broad view of the entire dock and market. There was a small Amerindian Museum inside, well-done and important (once again, and the Brazilians don't like to hear this), but the Indigenous population of Brazil was that of hunter-gatherers and nothing approaching the grandeur of Mexico, Guatemala, Honduras or Peru. Still, it served its purpose.

By now we were all soaking wet with sweat, hot and ready for a return to "Adventurer." Once again the shower water turned cool because of the demand; I heard comments but no complaints (except the ship grouch, now known to all, name withheld, a rich widow from Detroit who traveled the world with AT). A buffet lunch was available, time for an hour's rest and then the afternoon excursion. Everyone was exchanging notes at the lunch tables as all excursions were back on board, more to be said about that at CC in the p.m. and also, as mentioned earlier, tonight was the first "concert" on board by a "caboclo" band – the "country music" of the region, Eli our host and emcee.

I expected a very small group for my p.m. assignment, the Historic Area Churches, downtown, the Theatro da Paz, and the Basilica of Nazaré. But twenty hardy souls maybe wishing for an Indulgence for their "suffering" in that heat were into the two vans heading from anchorage just about fifteen minutes past the market we saw in the morning and to the tree-lined streets of old Belém. Everyone had extra bottled water and IA had arranged for stations along the way.

First stop was the old Jesuit Church where I got to tell (for the umpteenth time) the story of the Jesuits' forced exodus from Brazil and all the Spanish-Portuguese world in 1767, the result of the edict from the Marquis de Pombal of Portugal reflecting both secular and church politics of the times. Several adventurers, not necessarily Catholic, would ask me later over time on board about more of that story. But for then, the Jesuits were gone. Why? Church rivalry amongst the religious orders, jealousy perhaps because of extremely successful economic models in the Jesuit Missions in Southern Brazil and Paraguay. (We would show "The Mission" on board with Jeremy Irons and Robert de Niro, one of the trip favorites.) They established wonderful schools, mainly on the high school level, seminaries, hospitals but mainly missions for the conversion of Brazil's natives to the "True Faith." Plus, one of them did the first grammar of the Tupi Language (Brazilian natives' tongue) into the vernacular, Brazilian Portuguese. The Jesuit church's main merit was air conditioning. Its altars were that extravagant style of the Brazilian Baroque (17th-18 centuries) much like we would see in Bahia in a few days, altars with beautiful ornate carving of tropical woods, but unusual in that there was no gold gilt (no gold in the Amazon, El Dorado was never found).

We then moved just a short distance away to Belém's Cathedral, also air conditioned, with the long nave, many side altars and done in neo-classic because it was built in the very late 1700s and 1800s. We heard a choir practice of sorts, a half dozen acolytes accompanied by a very old organist, as creaky as his organ. Our folks were allowed to walk a few blocks through the commerce, noting the use of the "azulejos" those decorative tiles from the Peninsula, originally from the Arabs, used both on the façades of commercial buildings close to the waterfront as well as on many of the churches. We piled back into vans for the short ride to the main avenue and most beautiful of Belém, Avenida Presidente Getúlio Vargas, (Brazil's most famous and beloved president from the 1930s to the 1950s, more later on him) lined with old and huge mangueira trees (mangos), the large central park and then the crown jewel of Belém, its own Opera House, the "Theatro da Paz." Harry was once again in our group and added many inciteful comments that only a broad-based European historian was capable of, thus adding to the enjoyment of the trip. Our local guide this time was excellent, a degree in classical music as well as "Museumology" as they called it, Sônia Alvares. The next paragraph is all hers. An aside and something new for Gaherty the researcher: "cordel" now had made it to the regular newsstands along Avenida Getúlio Vargas, each small pamphlet encased in plastic and hanging in rows. As luck would have it, I met the poet re-stocking his story-poems, all the way from Paraíba on the east coast and traveling by airplane to the far west reaches of Brazil, Porto Velho in Rondônia. A big change from riding on the back of a burro or a second-class bus to the market in the early 20th century.

"The 'Theatro da Paz' was started in 1869 (well before Manaus's 'Teatro Amazonas' our guide wanted us to know) and modeled on 'La Scala' in Milan, strictly in the Neo-Classic style and opened in 1874. There are two important busts in the main entry hall – of José de Alencar and Gonçalves Dias, the main romantic period writers who introduced "Indianismo" to Brazilian Literature – and more important of Carlos Gomes, our great Opera composer. He is famous for 'O Guarani' based on an Alencar novel with an indigenous couple, our Romeo and Juliet, as the tragic main characters. It also has a wonderful ceiling mural based on the Greek Gods in the performance hall."

To me it was impressive but a "toned down" version of the "Teatro Amazonas;" maybe that would have changed had the time of their construction been reversed. Manaus and Belém competition was fierce and really a financial matter of life and death, fighting over the rubber proceeds and shipping. So the theaters reflect that, in my view. We lucked out with the visit with the Belém Chamber Orchestra doing a rehearsal of Romantic Period selections. It was then I met another of our adventurers, famous in her own right, a major symphonic orchestra conductor in Canada and the U.S. We would have much to talk about since she had conducted the "Concierto de Aranjuez" all over the western world, with major classic guitarists (I play amateur classic guitar, to come).

The final stop was one of Brazil's most important, but probably not known to foreigners – the Basilica of "Nossa Senhora de Nazaré" ["Our Lady of Nazareth"]. The story is a "hoot." A citizen found an image of the Virgin Mary with Infant beside a creek in that part of town, took it home and it kept showing up again at the original spot by the creek. A miracle! First a chapel, then a church, and then and now a huge Basilica (replete with miracles) marks the spot. More importantly it has become the largest, most grandiose religious holiday in Brazil, bigger than St. Francis in Canindé in the Northeast, Bonfim in Bahia, or Aparecida in São Paulo! The festival called "O Círio de Nazaré" lasts for one month! (I guess there isn't as much to do in Belém as Rio). I learned of it because one of the story-poems of "cordel" tells of the whole business, sacred and profane! And more, there's a connection to Portugal – the image is like the one in the seaside town of Nazaré, but, pardon, puts it in the shade. Oh, and that is what greets all the tourists, the long avenue with Mangueira trees (providing shade for the pilgrims) leading to the shrine. The church is beautiful even spectacular, but our adventurers are exhausted by now and badly in need of one of those cool showers.

CC that evening was lively, everyone talking of what they had seen that day, each trying to outdo the other. I'm saving the naturalists' tales for tomorrow night because by then everyone will have done the boat trip and the Goeldi - Zoo excursion. And the music performance has been postponed to tomorrow night, a normal "glitch" Eli says, but it will be our "goodbye" to the Amazon Region.

CC ended with all being called to another wonderful dinner and most folks to bed after a long day. Early call again tomorrow, so me too.

11

ADVENTURING IN BELÉM – II

July 7th. I'm thinking, if the rest of the trip, and we are barely started, is this interesting, it's going to be a big book. Oh, 5:30 a.m. again and time to roll out. Into the vans, 12 persons each, through the very poor part of Belém to the dock along the Guamá River. We passed canals with poor shacks on stilts, poverty all around. A different moment was a young boy on a bus we passed with a soccer ball cut in half for a hat!

We were greeted by Captain Henry of the "African Queen," a good name because it did remind of Humphrey Bogart's boat in Africa with Katherine Hepburn. My group could all fit on the boat and he started the engine and we left immediately veering into the strong current of the Guamá River. "The river was wide" (like the folksong) for miles until we turned into a tributary, then another, then yet another. By the last one the small river ran through a tunnel in the forest, a canopy of trees to either side and over the boat. Not being a naturalist nor a botanist (Kelly was with us) I can just recall a few points – hummingbirds, the famous "Rouxinol do Rio Negro" - a beautiful song bird I had seen, unfortunately, in bird cages in friends' houses in Rio and Bahia. The vegetation was interesting in that we saw for the first time "cacao" or "cocoa" trees mixed in the vegetation, not native to the area but brought up from Bahia decades ago.

There were no villages but just occasional "enclaves" of three or four houses, all on stilts, dugout canoes in front, fishing nets drying between coconut palms and always naked children playing in front. You would see a woman occasionally just peaking out from behind an open cabin window. Everything was made of wood. The captain said these "riverine" communities had been here for years and the people depended totally on fishing and their gardens of manioc flour. He didn't have many stories to tell other than a political diatribe against the corrupt State of Pará politicians who had forgotten the common people. He was definitely a pro-Military government man and against the Leftists in Belém (including the father of a serious girlfriend in Rio). The people we saw on this trip were black, descendants of slaves just barely surviving in the forest.

We rolled back into Belém two hours later; the honest and best thought I can give is of the immensity of that water world, truly without end. The Captain said it was the Guamá, the Pará and the hundreds of tributaries that provided that excess of fish, fruit and produce in the Ver O Peso market, hard to believe from what we saw this morning. I think most came from those fishing boats we saw at the market. Kelly had kept a running commentary mentioning perhaps two dozen plants she admitted to knowing and admitting there were so many more she had never seen.

After the return to the ship, cool showers, lunch and a nap we were out and about once again, this time to a famous place in a suburb of the city – the Emílio Goeldi Institute and Museum of Native Life and a botanical garden and zoo at its side. The Museum is unique, the best of its kind in this part of Brazil, tracing past and current day notions of the Amazon indigenous peoples, almost all hunter-gatherers, but with evidence that some migrated the entire distance of the Amazon River from Peru and Ecuador, an amazing feat. Tools, clothing, and cultural artifacts filled the museum.

I judge it was what was outside that thrilled the adventurers much more – tropical bromeliads, orchids, and finally - the huge "Umbrella Tree" that is the most famous in the Amazon Region. We had a guide with good English and she shared expertise with Kelly and us. It was the Kapok (Ceiba) tree capable of growing up to 200 feet in height, ten feet across at the trunk and a world in itself for its fruit, seeds, and animals and birds living in or around it. The thing we all noted is that its wood is terrific for dugout canoes, yet today the principal source of riverine travel other than the motor boats, and plenty of those were seen in this morning's excursion.

There were "caiman" or Amazon alligators, all kinds of birds including three different kinds of Toucans but the prize winner was a muscular "alpha male" rainforest jaguar or "onça" as they call it in Brazil. What a specimen! They have rosettes of spots (four or five or six with another in the center) and can be black (from my "Jungle Jim" Johnny Weissmuller movie days). They eat all those forest critters, deer, capybaras, and can swim like crazy – I read where they thump the water with their tail, imitating the fruit falling into the water and the Tambaqui fish waiting, and it's curtains for the fish. Supposedly they roam and hunt mainly at night, but don't take my word for it. Once again, I'm glad no one wanted to go for a swim back in the lagoon in Manaus.

That was enough for today; back to the ship in the air-conditioned vans, a rush to the showers and change of clothes and ready for CC and all the stories and Eli's music on board. If you add it all together there were about five intensive days in Manaus and Belém and I don't think anybody was disappointed. Kelly talked of the plants on the boat trip and orchids and bromeliads at Goeldi; Buck told us the difference between African Crocodiles and Amazon Alligators (neither being a desirable neighbor) and had great photos of that Jaguar in the zoo. I was approached by some of the Catholics wanting to know more about the Jesuits, Nazaré Basilica, and answered as best I could.

Also during CC Steve gave us a guide of what to expect the next three days on board. "Brazil is huge; there's much more to come, but we planned for this three-day hiatus after the Amazon for you to rest up, enjoy IA hospitality and education and fun. It will be almost three days before we dock again, but then it will get very busy and it's a whole new world coming up. We will have the talks as usual, yoga and exercise in the a.m., CC at 5:30, and special music presentations by Eli in the evening. We have a library of the best Brazilian films, documentary and commercial, and there will be one each night. Jack will be on the bow and the bridge in the mornings in case we see birds or whales. So I think we can all keep busy. Before I turn it over to Eli just a preview of tomorrow: in the a.m. Mike will give us an overview of Brazilian Culture, I will tell you about the oceans and currents off north and northeastern Brazil. In the p.m. Jack will have 'Birds of the Western Atlantic' and Harry will regale us with stories of the British and French History in the Americas. The weather is beautiful tonight so dinner will be on the back deck, still anchored for two hours, and Eli's music.

Dinner was IA's effort at a Belém specialty – "pato no tucupi" [roasted Amazon duck]. I had tasted it before but it was not my favorite in Brazil, so discretion and few words were in store. Things however were made mellow by IA's version of the Brazilian national drink – the caipirinha – two of those and you felt like dancing which is what Eli had in mind with a local quartet of "caboclo" or Pará country music. Sound box, guitar, flute and drums and singing of course. One Brazil "expert" on board (me) was hearing it for the first time. Adventurers however got with it and danced up a storm. After two hours the band left and IA took off on a beautiful moonlit night through Guarajá Bay, following the Pará river 100 kilometers to the ocean. We would stay off shore approximately twenty miles the entire journey, doing the max 20 knots on the "Road to Recife." It would be about 1400 nautical miles.

12

GETTING TO KNOW YOU

July 8th. I was up early at 6:30 with the mug of coffee from the Chart Room and the light breakfast of fruit, croissants and a piece of Chef Reynaldo's great chocolate cake, then to the room to review for the 9:00 a.m. talk. The phone jingled and it was Steve just checking in and wishing me well. Then again, a surprise call from Amy; she said she was so relieved for the break until Recife; there would be last minute stuff but all seemed to be coming together. She asked if we were still on for tonight and I assured her I was looking forward to it. "We've got a date for 9 p.m. Ok Mike? I'll check out your talk via closed circuit from the room at 9:00 this morning, so don't think I'm forgetting you."

There was a nice crowd in the lounge for the 9:00 a.m. talk, Willie ready in the audio-visual corner and away we went, my second talk but still without images, intentionally. These are the complete notes, all in the form of handouts. I warned them not to be frightened or head for the exits; I would just hit the highlights. It would be like a conversation with a lot of stories. And humor!

MIKE GAHERTY'S SECOND TALK: "BRAZILIAN CULTURE – INTRODUCTION AND A THUMBNAIL SKETCH"

Sources:

Brazil by its regions. Charles Wagley. Introduction to Brazil. Cultural Anthropology. 1960s

Politics: Thomas Skidmore

History: E. Bradford Burns

History from popular literature: Gaherty. "A Portrait of Twentieth Century Brazil – the Universe of the "Literatura de Cordel"

A. Language. Contrast Portugal and Brazilian (the Brazil Club T-Shirt – "Me dá um beijo – eu falo brasileiro"). In the U.S. we say "uhhh;" in Mexico: "este"; in Brazil "pois," but in Portugal it's "cãã." "RR" is trilled in southern Brazil, on TV, but otherwise aspirated: "h."

B. Religion - Roman Catholic and the rest
   African Spiritism
   Kardec Spiritism
   Protestants, Jews, Mormons, Native Spiritism

C. Architecture – for reference only as we travel.
   1. The "Brazilian Baroque:" Olinda and Recife/ Bahia and Its Churches /Ouro Preto/ Congonhas/ The Igreja da Glória and Mosteiro de São Bento in Rio.
   2. The 19th and Neo-Classical. Candelaria and "Teatro Municipal" and National Library in Rio (painting the national library). Public buildings in São Paulo.
   3. 20th century: New - São Paulo's "Edifício Copan", the modern in "Pampulha" in Belo Horizonte and Brasília. Brasília: Oscar Niemeyer, Lúcio Costa.

D. Race: 160 classifications. White, Black, "Pardo," "Caboclo," "Mulato," Asian.

E. Carnival. History and Description. Rio de Janeiro, Bahia, Recife, São Paulo, etc.
(My experiences Rio 1967: ten days seeing it all with friends; National "guests" were Jorginho Guinle, Gina Lollobrigida and Brigitte Bardot). All the clichés: 3 days' vacation; dreams of the poor, freedom. Numbers' racket; today's glitz and sex and skin. Satellite TV to the world.

F. Cuisine – the food. The "gringo" with the fragile stomach. "Canja de galinha," stories of warm "gerimum," "mel de açúcar e farofa; sarapatel, comida Baiana." Portuguese: "bacalhau, lulas" and Fado Music.
African: "azeite de dendê, cocada, abaré, acarajé, xinxim de galinha, moqueca de peixe, caruru."
Feijoada in Rio with Black beans. It tastes terrific going down.
Gaúcho: "churrasco"
Northeast Interior: "feijão mulato, charque, farofa, rapadura, peixe, sarapatel"
Amazon Region – "açaí, pato no tucupi, peixe"
Italian/ German/ Jewish and more
Fish – meat – vegetables – Brazil can grow anything!

G. The Visual Arts – For Reference Only
  1. Painting: Anita Malfaldi, Cândido Portinari, Di Cavalcanti; Museum of Art in São Paulo
  2. Sculpture: Aleijadinho in Ouro Preto and Congonhas do Campo
  3. Landscaping: Roberto Burle Marx (Gaherty went to the beach.)

H. Literature - For reference only: Padre Anchieta, Gregório de Matos, Castro Alves, José de Alencar, Machado de Assis Euclides da Cunha, Semana de Arte Moderna em São Paulo, Mário de Andrade, Carlos Drummond de Andrade, Gilberto, Freyre, Romancistas do Nordeste (Graciliano Ramos, José Lins do Rego, Jorge Amado

Raquel de Queiróz), Érico Veríssimo, Dias Gomes, Clarice Lispector, João Guimarães Rosa, João Cabral de Melo Neto, Ariano Suassuna

(Gaherty's favorite: Luís Fernando Veríssimo and his Chronicles).

But Brazilians complain that "nobody reads."

Cultural Institutions: Brazilian Academy of Letters, National Library (and the painting thereof), Dom Pedro II Museum in Petrópolis, State of São Paulo Symphony; the Universities: NE, Rio, São Paulo

I. Folklore: Dances, Festivals, etc." Gaherty's special interest: "literatura de cordel." More later on this.

J. Sports: "futebol." In Gaherty's "Adventures" see the Carioca championship, and then, Pelé and Santos at the Maracanã in Rio.

K. Popular culture-mass culture. The "Telenovelas." Priests changed the hour of mass in parts of Brazil. Glória Pérez, daughter Daniella: life imitates the "novela."

L. Performing artists – music. Eli's expertise once again as we get on down the way.

Heitor Villa Lobos / Dorival Caymmi/João Gilberto/ Antônio Carlos Jobim/ Chico Buarque de Holanda/ /Jair Rodrigues/

Nara Leão/ Vinicius de Morais/ Roberto Carlos/ Sertanejo music – seresteiros/ Axé/ Pagode/ Caetano Veloso e Tropicália/ all the samba/ folk: milonga from Rio Grande do Sul/ "cantoria" from Northeast.

M.Cinema: "Black Orpheus!"/ "Cinema Novo" and Glauber Rocha/ Fernanda Montenegro/ The Barreto Family Producers and cinema based on literary works. (Jorge Amado)

For all those left out, "sinto muito," a nearly impossible task. Maybe you will remember the anecdotes. "Obrigado." Mike Gaherty

It might all seem too much to handle, but, once again, all the above was given to everyone in handouts. They understood a professor has to do this, but I reminded there would be no exams and just for their records. A few later said they were invaluable souvenirs of the trip; others left the handouts on the tables for scratch paper or in the waste baskets on the way out. C'est la vie. We can't all be Naturalists! The talk involved lots of quips, jokes and laughter; it went well. Applause at the end. What mattered most to me was Leonel and friends all came up and were effusive in their compliments "Como poderia um estrangeiro saber tanto do Brasil?" I had a "cafezinho" with them before the next talk and quizzed them on the experience so far. No complaints except that they were a bit taken aback over the general lack of knowledge of the adventurers about Brazil. I attempted to make light of it saying "That's why they're here, and me too!" Laughter.

Steve's talk at 11:00 was highly technical but a terrific overview of ocean currents, winds and even fisheries for the next 1500 sea miles. The nature lovers, and veterans of AT's ocean travel throughout the planet loved it. For me it was all new, a bit scientific (not my forte) but welcome.

Lunch was tasty, a smorgasbord of salads, pastas, fish dishes in sauce, and sandwich makings if you chose. Of course, an array of desserts to follow, great Brazilian demitasse coffee ("cafezinhos"). Most folks had time for a nap before the afternoon talks.

Jack Bataldi's talk was exciting and a bit overwhelming. Like I mentioned he has a bird list of over 5000, and I don't know how many of the images were original, but all the naturalists came with scanned images from many sources. He reviewed the birds from the Amazon, all those songbirds, parrots and macaws, and then the general types of seabirds we might see on the trip, and then the ones in this region. I tried to take notes just on their names so I could look them up in bird books or encyclopedias at home; I'm sure I missed some, but the main word was it was beautiful!

Harry Downing's second talk, slightly off course from the "Adventurer's" but highly valuable to all of us, was an overview of British and French colonization in the New World, mainly the U.S. Colonies and Canada, but with a smidgen of notes on the Caribbean and the old Guianas. (I interjected a question and commentary afterwards on the role of England and Isla San Andrés off Colombia, what I saw as the "Microcosm of the Caribbean.") Harry noted he would have a bit to say about Brazil and the British role in the building of the railroads (me too) and the large British role in Argentina later on when we were to get closer to that part of South America. There was terrific audience response first because they knew a lot more about it, secondly because of a wealthy French restauranteur from Quebec on board with friends. As might be expected he did not see eye to eye with Harry vis a vis the Indian Wars and final "solution" in Canada.

A passing note, Mr. Diderot, a distant descendant of Denis Diderot of the Encyclopédie, and I got on famously for a lot of reasons, certainly not for my lack of knowledge of French and France. The French have always thought Brazil exotic, have loved Carnival in Rio and all of Brazil's culture. We would have glasses of fine French wine after I showed "Black Orpheus" later on, with Marcel Camus' role, and we would laugh over Brigitte Bardot's adventures in Brazil and Jean Paulo Belmondo's in "Our Man in Rio" from the 1950s. He came up to me after the culture talk when

I mentioned Brigitte and wondered if we met (saying all this with a sparkle in his eye and a wink). He became one of my favorite adventurers, spending several meals and some time in CC with me. Dinner tonight was with him and his wife and talking of the things mentioned; always a treat, he knew the finest French wines and would share them at dinner.

"THE NAKED JUNGLE"

After dinner we showed "The Naked Jungle" with Charlton Heston and Eleanor Parker and the "marabunta" or Army Ants. Heston's "cocoa plantation in the Amazon" was threatened by a huge swath of migrating "marabunta" ants. Kelly hosted, saying to remember it was just Hollywood, but a good yarn and she had fun counting ants. Everyone got a big kick out of it and especially when reassured by Kelly there would not be any ant migrations the rest of the trip (but maybe some giant termite mounds and leaf cutter ants).

I could sit in the back of the lounge and eased out right after the movie, on time to Amy's room at 9:00 p.m. She was at her desk and had just got off the phone with the people from the Pernambuco Tourist Commission (Recife) setting up the local guides for our long two days and one night stay there. "I'm ready for a drink," and she pulled a bottle of Chivas and ice out of her private "frigobar" – "Executive Privilege Mike, you better keep on my good side. So, have you survived and how are you doing?" (She got up, put her arms around me, snuggled up a bit, and offered a warm kiss.) It had been a long time since Brazil adventures in "Letters III" and Molly in New York, but there was nothing wrong with my reaction as Amy laughed and commented.

"It has been exciting and great fun, but not perfect. As much as I like the Amazon, the forest and the critters and the heat are not my cup of tea. I'll be a lot more relaxed in Recife, Bahia and on down to Rio. I'm learning the ropes on the 'Adventurer' and everyone has been nice. But how about you? I want to hear more of your routine and am really curious how you got along in that year in Rio."

"No disasters yet, and they do happen Mike; things are lining up for Recife and I've begun the Bahia sector; Rio will come later. Incidentally thanks for your input on Recife; AT was not aware of some of the excursion possibilities, so you are on the hook for that. I haven't read your 'Letters' Series yet, but know you had 'a girl in every port' in 'Adventures;' I'm hoping a girl from back home can interest you as well? Mike, I had a great time in Rio, worked extremely hard at the GF Foundation, but girls do want to have fun, right? There was a bevy of up and coming Brazilian young guys willing to show me Rio, and it did get a bit intense with one of them. We did the beach scene, the restaurant scene, Carnival in February and he even took me to meet his family in São Paulo. We saw the Museum of Art of São Paulo, ate great meals and I got to see a slice of big business life in the city. I decided SP was not for me and we actually "cooled it" some back in Rio. The schooling was fantastic and helped me to no end to do my job here with AT. So here we are."

I brought Amy up to date on my research and time in Brazil the last two years. She was on the ships when all the business with Chico, the "Censura Prévia" ["Prior Censorship"] and "Mistakes of Our Youth" LP and concerts happened. I mentioned that because of support for Chico, his protest music and reports to the NYT that the "dis-invite" came. We spent the next half hour with another drink, listening to some "Bossa" music and, well, getting to know each other. Better. She said, "Let's do this again after Recife. I'll see if I can get on your van for the Xangô ceremony." Kisses, hugs and a goodnight followed.

13

PASSING FORTALEZA AND THE "COPACABANA" OF THE NORTH

July 9th. Another entire day at sea. Ho hum. Not really. The naturalists shared the morning with birds and sea critters, Steve did an update telling us about the North and South Atlantic Currents and Trade Winds and how the Portuguese seafarer Pedro Álvares de Cabral was blown off course on his way to the East Indies in 1500 and ended up discovering Brazil! Some adventurers asked why we were not stopping in Fortaleza, a very large city on the north coast of Brazil, growing in size, importance and the economy of Brazil. Captain Tony did consent to going in just less than two miles off shore to see the row of skyscrapers of what the Cearenses like to call "The Copacabana of the North." I piped up that we would see more beaches than you could want in the coming two weeks, so just hold on.

Early in the p.m. I was given a chance to do a "short" talk on Northeastern Culture and folklore, modestly my "forte" in Brazil. It was and is not the main talk I'll do on all that but I did note its importance in the State of Ceará and very nearby Fortaleza. First was the up to that time most famous female writer of Brazil, the novelist Raquel de Queiróz from the interior of the State. Then I explained that the "literatura de cordel" the story-poems of Northeastern Brazil came from Portugal and were a mainstay for entertainment and news for the rural and city customers in the markets and fairs most of the 20th century. There were many poets in Fortaleza but the main place in Ceará State was two hundred miles south where Father Cícero Romão Batista lived and did "miracles" from 1879 to 1934. He became among the half-dozen most popular characters in "cordel" and lived in a tiny burg in an oasis in the drought-stricken state of Ceara (famous for the "Drought of the Two 77s," killing one million people in 1877 in the 19th century). I did a "pilgrimage" to his town Juazeiro to buy story-poems from the largest "cordel" press in the Northeast, saw his tomb, shrine and house and visited the "miracle room" where harpies accosted me for coins to "Tell the story of Padim Cícero." I left it at that for now.

Gino arranged a "cook's tour" later in the p.m. which included an opportunity to see the laundry world, the kitchen and cold storage and the ship's ultra-modern methods of disposal of garbage and waste, etc. In all honesty it was great, giving us all a chance, and me for the first time, to see the "nuts and bolts" of a smooth-running ship. We did not make it down to the depths with engines etc. (too hot down there and smelly the Captain said).

CC was congenial and highlighted by Eli's first on-board music presentation – an overview of Brazilian music from the North and Northeast, what we would experience in Pernambuco. I'm not sure how the adventurers took to it because it is strange with the heavy spoken accent of the interior of the Northeast, home incidentally of much of my research on the story-poems. (I would talk more about all that tomorrow before the late-night arrival to Recife). Eli talked of the "baião" or as some incorrectly call it, the "samba" of the Northeast. He had a good video on "Forró" as the music was called and its most famous composer-singer "Luíz Gonzaga." The music is normally a machine-gun rrrrr fast with voice, accordion or sound box, triangle and drums. I stood up, grabbed Amy and we gave an ersatz demonstration of how you can dance to it (kind of like a gringo two-step) and many adventurers followed. I think most considered it Brazil's version of "country music" and that's all right. The IA bartender was happy as adventurers opened their ample pocketbooks for that top shelf happy-hour stuff.

We filed in to dinner shortly thereafter (always after tidying up the lounge), Amy intentionally heading to a different table than I, "good PR," she says." I sat with new people, a real hoot, ex – New Yorkers, Jewish by ethnicity, and we began a long series of conversations and fun dealing mainly with some of the best comedians and writers and actors in NY and Hollywood history. One of the gentlemen ran an optics shop on Madison Avenue and came "that close" to getting the contract for prescription snorkeling and diving goggles for Jacques Cousteau (he didn't get it only because of a shipping snafu to Cousteau's boat). Mel Brooks was the main item of conversation. Dinner was my kind – filet mignon, baked potato, Caesar salad, an icy Xingu beer and vanilla ice cream and chocolate sauce for dessert. How patriotic can you be? Except for the beer.

Tomorrow would be our last day "at sea" before arriving in Recife late evening. I had specifically suggested to AT to add Recife to the itinerary and suggested the activities so as Amy said, I "was on the hook" for all that. There would be a one-hour introduction to Recife at 4:00 p.m. just before CC tomorrow night. A lot to cover, definitely one of the high points on the trip for me and I hope for others.

14

BRAZIL'S NORTHEAST –
RECIFE, ANOTHER WORLD

July 10th. We passed Natal on the bulge of Brazil during the night, interesting for some of the adventurers because it was the location of a U.S. Army Air Force Base for two years in the early 1940s, always in conjunction with Brazil's government, of the air shuttle of planes, supplies and personnel to the Front in Northern Africa in the battle against Mussolini's troops in Ethiopia, and Germany and Rommel's Panzers in northern Africa. They took off from Natal and flew for refueling at the archipelago of Fernando de Noronha about 225 miles east and then on to Dakar in French West Africa. Of even more importance even on this trip was Brazil's role as ally and participant in the Battle for Italy under General Mark Clark in 1944, and more yet, the officers of that campaign were the leaders instrumental in Brazil's Revolution of 1964 and the ensuing dictatorship to this date of 1972.

Around three in the p.m. we passed another large northeastern city, the capital of the State of Paraíba, João Pessoa, but with no plans to stop there either, keeping our eye on the goal of Recife, "The Venice of Brazil" for some, "The Calcutta of Brazil" for others, a major historical and cultural place in Brazil for Gaherty and the IA adventurers.

The talks that day were again interesting, first in the a.m. was Buck Weylander with a talk harking back a bit to the Amazon, but really as a point of departure – Big Cats of the Rain Forest and Northern Brazil. He had magnificent images of the jaguar like we saw in the zoo in Belém, but more in depth and with videos of the jaguar hunting prey in the rain forest. He then surprised most people I think by talking of the "lion" of the backlands of Brazil's northeast – what we in the U.S. would say is a cougar or mountain lion. The latter is common, feeds on deer but also goats, sheep and stray or sick cattle in the dry backlands. I chimed in with the story-poems of the "Literatura de Cordel" and their main heroes, the cowboys and the "valiant back landers" who aside from chasing and bringing in wild horses and wild bulls also had to fend off attacks of the occasional cougar. And the heroics of back landers doing the "travessia" or odyssey of crossing the dry backlands in their migration to the coast or to the south to avoid the droughts and fend off an occasional lion. Buck ended with the images of the greatest wildlife area of Brazil, the west – central "Pantanal" the place most known for the "onças."

A second talk was Harry Downing again this time the competition of the Portuguese, the French and the Dutch for dominance in Brazil dating from the late 1500s, from Rio in the south, Belém on the Amazon but the most important the Dutch Invasion and rule in the "Dutch Northeast" and Recife until 1640. Holland in effect won over and took over Portuguese Brazil from Recife all the way to Fortaleza. Their role had grown with the weakening of the Portuguese Crown with the death of King Sebastião in 1578 and no successor to the throne, so by default to the Spanish Hapsburgs who already had enough to worry about. The Dutch were inextricably connected to the ethnic Jews of Amsterdam, Northeast Brazil, Dutch Guiana and Caribbean islands and eventually New York City. Since we had several Jewish people on board the talk became quite animated with questions, Harry's response came, and an invitation for me to join in with experience in Recife. I said I did have interaction with Jewish intellectuals at the Joaquim Nabuco Research Center in the 1960s and was a very good friend of Columbia Fulbrighter Paul Goldberg doing research on the sugar cane industry in the Northeast, but no more. (It made me think to do a little prep on that subject for later.) The conflict which ended in 1654 with the Battle of Guararapes in Pernambuco forced out the Dutch but with them much scientific progress and development of the sugar cane industry, and the Jewish contribution was not small. Even then it was indigenous and black troops which largely enabled the Portuguese crown to win back the Northeast.

After a break and afternoon tea and goodies we started CC earlier that day, at 5:00 p.m. and I had the floor for the introduction to Recife and the Northeast from a cultural point of view. Harry had covered much of the history. I told of the origin of the name of the city – Recife – due to the miles long, straight as an arrow reef running parallel to the coast south of the city. The original center in the 16th and 17th centuries before Recife grew was Olinda and we would spend a lot of time there (I mentioned my own introduction living in a painters' atelier in 1966). The old colonial three story mansions ["sobrados"] and churches, the picturesque scene with tall palms and the hills overlooking that beautiful ocean and down the hill ten kilometers to Recife.

I mentioned its cultural importance with major writers from colonial days to the 19th century Romantics and the leaders in the Abolition of Slavery finally in 1888, then the major role of sociologist Gilberto Freyre of Columbia U. in New York and his master's thesis "The Masters and the Slaves" – his fame and his founding of the Joaquim Nabuco Institute on his family's sugar cane plantation (Freyre was part of the "sugar cane aristocracy" of the Northeast, sugar cane being then and still today the major agricultural crop, sharing importance now with industrialization).

Then I introduced everyone to another of its major facets: the link to folklore, Afro-Brazilian religion, and themes of folk-popular poetry, the importance of local markets and fairs, the sub-culture and the saga of the back landers fighting the droughts and the major wave of migration to Rio and São Paulo, religious fanaticism and the real banditry of 19th and 20th century Brazil. A link would be the "Casa de Cultura" excursion tomorrow – a major prison in NE Brazil where Graciliano Ramos one of Brazil's "Novelists of the Northeast" was held and where one of the most famous bandits Antônio Silvino served a long term as a model prisoner and made enough from prison tasks to educate his children through primary school, no small feat in the Northeast. There was much more, but I think it whetted their appetites (speaking of that they could get northeastern regional food on the "Casa" tour tomorrow); we would see several of the high points linked to this cultural history the next two days. Not the least would be the role of the ocean, the reef, the beaches and beach life in Recife and the coast north and south. Tomorrow night I would clue them in to "Xangô."

Dinner was delightful as usual, and I ended sitting with two of the naturalists, Buck and Kelly, and some adventurers from Boston. They of course were familiar with the New Bedford Whaling Museum and its history and were looking forward to a chance of seeing whales at Abrolhos after Salvador. They spoke glowingly of seeing the pink dolphins outside of Manaus and the fish markets and stories by all. Buck and Kelly added anecdotes from past AT trips; both had many stories of whales in Alaska and along the Oregon Coast. Buck said Abrolhos could be "iffy," but Captain Tony assured it would be a good time to be there, whales having their calves and getting them to a good start before the return trip to Antarctica. But we would be "in the middle of a very large ocean." He added that Portugal's role in whaling and seafaring also extended to the archipelago of Madeira and a world-renowned whaling museum on the outskirts of Funchal. For me it was a trip back to the room to prepare for the Recife tours tomorrow and CC tomorrow night.

15

RECIFE AND ENVIRONS

July 11th. Boa Viagem Beach. Amy had arranged the next morning for vans to take everyone to Boa Viagem Beach south of Recife for swimming, sun bathing, snorkeling and if they wanted, a "jangada" fishing boat ride. We were all forewarned however, to not venture too close to the reef and certainly not to go to it or beyond, but that was not a problem as the reef was almost one mile out into the ocean. I joked with the male staffers and adventurers, "We're not in Rio yet; this is the old Northeast; you will see a lot of skin and good looking 'nordestinas' but in a 'maiô' [Maillot] or one – piece bathing suit. The old conservative, Catholic Northeast still considers the bikini a little too advanced. There are perhaps 'better' beaches all up and down the coast today, but Boa Viagem is still nice and gives us the 'big picture' of Recife and the region."

"Recife Turismo" would have a guide with each group (doubling as security); we were told to take no valuables and not to have the locals "watch" our stuff when we swam, but rather one of our group. Pickpockets abound at the beach and gringos are "filet mignon." I explained in the van that even up to a few years ago it was amazing that many Recifenses did not know how to swim but would just wade waist high in the warm pools of clear water close in. We could choose that, but there would be plenty of room for the swimmers and snorkelers to go farther out, the latter a little more liable to see sea life closer to the reef, but Recife had a large cadre of life guards with life savers on ropes for emergencies. Sharks were on an occasional basis but once again the waters were cleared if there was a sighting. (I saw a bloated white body float up on another beach in 1966, shark attack.)

I warned a good sun screen was a great idea. All kinds of vendors were there with soft drinks, beer, "limonada" and snacks. And it was an education to see the coconut stands along the beach sidewalk and the fellows with razor sharp machetes ready to slice one open for you, and if you wanted a local treat (which I did not recommend) they would pour in a generous dollop of sugar cane rum. I noted it was a hazardous profession, many of the vendors with less than all their digits.

Maria Farinha Sand Crab

And from many months' previous Boa Viagem experience I encouraged everyone to watch for the "Maria Farinhas" - white sand crabs all along the beach. These would come out of their hole, wave their antennae and scoot off sideways down the beach (Buck scooped up two or three and brought to the ship, promising to release them the next day).

What was most unique for adventurers and Recife was a chance to ride (for a very reasonable price) on one of the now tourist "jangadas." These were the original fishing boats for the most modest of "nordestinos," made from four balsa logs tied together and with a makeshift six foot "mast" for the sail. The main fishing boats for hundreds of years in northeast and north Brazil, coming from the Indians, they could fly at amazing speeds with a good wind, and there was lots of wind. Several of the adventurers including myself and Amy did the ride. (Have I said how good she looked in an emerald green maillot?)

And lastly for those inclined, folks could join the locals (for a nice donation) in a pickup "futbol" contest (soccer game); the entire north beach up to Pina was marked off for amateur soccer leagues on the weekends. Many did so.

Willie was up to something, we did not know what, but with scuba gear he hitched a ride on a "jangada" and went almost out to the reef for a dive. We would see the results at CC later that day. All agreed that this beach experience was a novelty and great fun; I assured them that Salvador would offer a different scene and especially Rio on down the way. It was "um sucesso" – a big success.

Adventurers were given the option to stay at Boa Viagem and enjoy one of the delicious local seafood lunches, but to be back by 1:30 to clean up and get ready for the p.m. tour. Oh, just an aside, Recife was full of parks, tropical trees and more, as well as Olinda (later) but we were warned that the Botanical Garden – Zoo was a disaster, poorly funded, in horrible disarray with near-starving animals, and all these in old 19th century cages. We said there were better days ahead, in fact fantastic birding and animals to come down the coast in the next few days. There was some grousing, but the naturalists would be along in Olinda tomorrow and that would bring surprises or as they put it – "good spots."

The p.m. offered something different for adventurers – a folk art market in a real, historic prison – then something familiar – a gold gilt chapel with all its excess – and then a wonderful music show on the back deck with a barbecue, icy beer or "caipirinhas" and a lot of dancing. Here's what happened.

2:00 p.m. If you count the actual docks at Recife one crosses three rivers from where the "Adventurer" is docked to get to the mainland across from the final one, the Capibaribe. (Recalling the cliché of Recife as "The Venice of Brazil," I suppose so in a manner of words.) That is the route of our vans with me commenting in one of them on how I walked those streets and crossed those bridges almost every work day, Monday to Friday, for six months straight in 1966. I've written all the details in "Adventures" – the bandaged beggars on the bridges, the adventures at the Post Office with the glue pots and surly clerks, with the illegal street vendors and the "fuzz," the twice a week jaunt to the old São José Market to buy the story - poems of "cordel," listen to poets "sing" and sell their poetry, and the once a week walk to USIS to get my mail. Our destination this p.m. was across the Capibaribe River, not far from the Law School of Pernambuco and my former boarding house euphemistically called "The Rose House," and "watering hole," "The Academic Bar." Adventurers in the van said all should hear these stories and to repeat them at CC tonight. Okay. Traffic was heavy, the end of the "noon" rush hour when Pernambucanos still head home and back for the big noon meal, the main meal of the day, and a nap for many. There is so much to say: across the river from the "Casa de Cultura" is the modest hotel where I stayed for the first night in Recife in 1966, and down the way the famous "Restauante Leite" where one of the most infamous of all political acts took place in Brazil in 1930 when the vice presidential candidate under Getúlio Vargas, João Pessoa, was assassinated, the victim of backlands crony politics. And it was crime that took me first to the now "Casa de Cultura."

This major tourist site in Recife with over 150 shops with regional handicrafts from every part of the state was originally a major prison in Pernambuco, dating from 1850. In the form of a cross, next to the Capibaribe, it kept one of the cells in original form, pretty grizzly. One of Brazil's most famous novelists Graciliano Ramos from Alagoas was imprisoned there after being accused of being a Communist, this in the 1930s. Released, he and his fame grew, a member of the four elite

"Novelists of the Northeast" (one we mentioned from Ceará, Raquel de Queiróz, another José Lins do Rego the son of a sugar cane baron in Paraíba, and a third we shall talk much about, Jorge Amado, Brazil's most famous writer, from Salvador). The other prisoner was important to me and to Pernambuco history – the real life bandit Antônio Silvino from the neighboring state of Paraíba, termed the "Robin Hood" of the Northeast, captured finally after twenty years in the late teens of the 20th century, he was imprisoned, became a model prisoner and with the modest prisoner earnings from making handicrafts, put his children through public grade school. He is one of the major heroes of the story-poems of "cordel" and some chapbooks were for sale in the market. Adventurers with a sturdy stomach could also try many regional foods. I daresay these people were world travelers and curious to know all cultures, and many tried the regional foods. Not yours truly. Sorry.

Just across town, a short van ride (with air conditioning) was Recife's crown jewel in churches and religious art, and there were many, hard to choose – the "Capela de Ouro" [Golden Chapel], our second and last stop of the afternoon. Begun in 1696 by the Third Order of Franciscans, lay people who happened to be rich from the prosperous sugar cane economy, the chapel was built for the novices in the Franciscan seminary. Today it is part of a complex with the Church of St. Anthony, a religious art museum and patio. The name comes from the highly intricate carved wood altars, statues and ceilings covered in gold. Huge mural paintings were on the ceiling as well. In addition, the balance of the walls is composed of panels of the famous blue tiles – azulejos – famous from Portugal and Spain and earlier from the Arabs, much more to be seen in Salvador and Rio. Most adventurers had been to Europe and seen the grandeur of its churches and palaces, but marveled at this in the New World.

A small anecdote but worthy of mention, it was on a visit to the chapel on a day of tourism with my friend, engineer and sugar cane mill wizard and his fiancée that I actually served as chaperone to the couple! Another example of northeastern social mores and manners yet in the 1960s. He was in his late 20s, she in her early 20s! Try that in Boston or New York!

Everyone was weary from the outings and glad to get back to "Adventurer" where we had a wonderful on – board concert by one of Eli's finds: Flávio Campos's eleven-piece musical group specializing in original and folk recreations of music of the region. Classic guitar, three kinds of flute, violin and Arabic "rabeca," accordion and sound box and several types of drums and base fiddle made for a sophisticated, stylized version of music from Pernambuco and Paraíba States. And one could dance, members of the group taking turns in demonstrating the "baiao" and the main dance, the "frevo." Several guests then took part, and I wheeled Amy out once more. Cocktails were available and indeed may have provided some incentive to all.

That evening a special presentation by all the naturalists showed us the animals and birds of the region plus Willie's surprise from the Reef – a rather large octopus in a glass case – his story of it and all the tropical fish he filmed and showed us. "Ollie" would be released tomorrow a.m. close to the reef. I did a twenty-minute preview of Olinda, emphasizing Xangô, the Afro-Brazilian religious rite tomorrow night. Thus ended day one in Recife amidst great enthusiasm by all. I think day two would be equally exciting.

16

RECIFE AND OLINDA – SUGAR CANE, COLONIAL SPENDOR AND AFRICA'S CONTRIBUTION – XANGÔ

July 12th. A few adventurers stayed on the ship this morning saying they wanted to rest before the late p.m. and big night ahead in Olinda, but those of us who ventured out experienced a big slice of Brazil's economic and social history. The vans took us to the Joaquim Nabuco Social Science Research Center in far west Recife where we were welcomed by an acquaintance of mine from research days, the Head of the Institute, Mauro Mota, and shown around by his son Roberto also a friend from 1966. The Institute was founded by a famous Brazilian, Gilberto Freyre, a son of the sugar cane aristocracy, and built from a converted "Big House" or mansion of sugar cane owners. What I wanted adventurers to see was the entire exterior side of the main administration building and auditorium all in Portuguese blue tile and the massive wooden staircase leading to the second floor as well as the wooden floors themselves- all out of Brazilian hardwoods and rosewood, not unlike the Opera House in Manaus. This was the grandeur of "The Masters and Slaves."

To the side was the Sugar Museum where one of my main informants on the story-poems, the son of the "empresario" of "cordel" for almost forty years, João Martins de Atayde, was doing an internship. The museum had it all, some a bit technical for some of us, but the story and recreation of a 19th century sugar mill in the Northeast (replete with the big grinding wheel and oxen). I saw and reported on the series of "fazendas" or plantations of one of the most famous sugar cane families, that of the novelist José Lins do Rego in Paraíba. Everyone seemed interested but my ethnic Jewish friends in particular who knew the role of Jews for sixty years in the 17th century. There was a trio of adventurers from Louisiana, New Orleans to be exact, and they knew the role of sugar cane there. Incidental to this was slavery; the labor until 1888 was black slaves and from then to the present their "free" descendants and poor white and mixed blood small farmers from the Northeast interior.

Recife from Olinda

The schedule for the day was inverted due to on-shore plans: we had the main meal from noon to 2 p.m. (late night snacks and drinks at 11:00 p.m.

ship departure at 11:30 p.m.), a long break to rest or whatever, and then a departure at 4:00 p.m. to travel to the original capital of the "Capitania" in the 16th century (huge Brazil was split into "captaincies" in the 16th and 17th century, akin to our colonies or later states, Pernambuco the richest for 100 years), really a "suburb" of modern Recife. Olinda [Oh! Beautiful"] now split into modern and "historic" is known for its seven hills full of tropical plants and palm trees. The sugar barons built their mansions and churches and lived the good life for 400 years. We visited many including the Benedictine Monastery (a joke of modern Brazil – "filled with Nazi refugees making beer in modern Brazil.")

There was a two-hour break at one of the beautiful bar-cafés overlooking the view down to Recife, and or free time until 8:00 p.m., all meeting once again at the "Vista do Mar" Restaurante. In the shade of the palm trees and with a cool ocean breeze it was absolutely delightful. Many adventurers took advantage and went for walks through the cobblestone ("paralelepípedo" the Portuguese name) streets, seeing more mansions, the many shops and art galleries. I and most of the staff sat with some guests and ordered those liter bottles of "Brahma Choppe" and "Antarctica" beers famous in Brazil (the place had very decent restrooms, not always the case in Brazil). We were not particularly hungry but they offered a huge shrimp cocktail, crab meat and dip, and chips along with the beer. We ended up trying it and trying it again.

Xangô in Olinda

Then came the "pièce de resistance" of Recife, a pre-arranged (for a price) visit by all to the "terreiro" or religious meeting house of Pai Edu (Father of the Saint and Cult Leader) in Olinda. It was here I was introduced to Xangô in 1966 in a memorable and a bit frightening night. Pai Edu had reluctantly changed his meeting time to 8 p.m. instead of 10 p.m. with the understanding we would leave before 11:00 (he and members would continue into the wee hours of the night and early morning). I had explained the rudiments of this major Afro-Brazilian Religious variant on board yesterday. It was a major topic of my Fulbright study in 1966-1967 but not the first, that being "cordel." In very capsulated form here it is:

Xangô is along with "candomblé" in Bahia the major Afro – Brazilian religious variant in all Brazil. It is all very complicated business but suffice to say, although distantly related to "voodoo" or "santería" in Cuba, it is far more sophisticated and beautiful. Pai Edu and other leaders recognized that their fellow Brazilians and certainly foreign tourists wanted to know and experience this religion, so they "compromised" by allowing visitors and tourists to many ceremonies. That is, far from all the ceremonies, for there are many secret ones, particularly initiation ceremonies which I have witnessed. How to summarize it? There is a pantheon of gods, called by various names like "saints," "gods," "enchanted ones" and more, originating in religious practice in Africa. Catholic Portugal forced the slaves to convert to Catholicism (we shall see much of this in Salvador), but it was a veneer. They hid their true allegiance to the African gods by giving them Catholic saints' names, Oxala (God the Father), Iemanjá (the Virgin Mary and dozens of others. The basic religious ceremony is a session of chants (in Nagô, the African language), songs, and dances. The members of the cult, mainly women dressed in finery with billowing skirts, turbans and necklaces and bracelets, but not all, fall into what foreign scholars call a trance, but not them. They believe that each Xangô member has a saint or patron saint and that saint comes down during the session and takes possession of them. Then they dance with steps known to the saint and imitate the saint, communing with her or him. These same saints have their own mode of dress, their way of dancing, their food and drink favorites. They can bless you and heal you, and in some cases, put a hex on you. That is the essence of what we experienced that evening, with a surprise or two.

At the height of the possessions, one of the lady adventurers fell into trance and fainted. Brought to quickly by the gentle hands of one of the "daughters" of the saints, she recovered but was happy (and admitted to me privately later that she practiced a variant of the religion on New York's upper east side). More than that, two persons, both French, a man and woman, were "slain in the spirit" as well. Some of our group were frightened, the room grew very hot, all the participants sweating heavily. At one point our guide and Steve our AL nodded to me that we should all leave, and we all respectfully walked out of the hall, our guide speaking to one of the "oguns" or "administrators" and handing him an envelope I surmised was full of cash. I bowed to Pai Edu, thanking him and congratulating him on the evening. He in turn nodded in appreciation and went on with the ritual. I neglected to say that in 1967 I would hear the drums of Xangô throughout the night until dawn two or three times a week in my corner hammock in the atelier in Olinda.

I think I can safely say that up to this point, the ceremony was the highlight of the trip, albeit, aside from nature. This was something AT could offer and remain an indelible memory for the adventurers. Back on board in the dining hall dining staff served delicious sandwiches, fruit and chocolate and coconut desserts, and most people had wine and other libations, all excitedly talking of their experience. Steve and Amy came up to me, smiling and with a handshake or embrace and said this alone proved my worth on the trip. I said, "And so much more to come!"

I had a late-night drink in Amy's room and she admitted she never had experienced anything like this in her tenure in Rio. I assured her there could be surprises there as well. I probably stayed a bit too long, but we both were enjoying each other's company.

I think most all adventurers and staff conked out for some sound sleep, once again exhausted by what we had seen and done. Two days of "At Sea" would be a respite. It would be 500 plus nautical miles and with a pleasant but not top speed we would arrive in Salvador at noon in two days.

17

AT SEA TO BAHIA

July 13th. Once again after those intense two days in Recife, "at – sea" routine was welcome. That meant early morning stretching and workout for the early risers (and many of the Thai staff used this time for weight work), and the true birders up on the bridge kibitzing with Jack, Buck and sometimes Kelly (see Jack's report to follow). Over such a long trip there was great rapport – adventurers and ornithologists got to know each other well; and "Adventurer" captain's crew were available as well. I made it up there only sporadically – if there was a call or spotting of whales or the like. This early a.m. I was preparing my third official talk – "Religion in Brazil" – requested by Jack to explain what we saw and what would be coming in Salvador. But not before the mug of coffee from the chart room and those goodies at the "early – bird breakfast."

Masked Boobies

9:00 a.m.
First talk: "Seabirds of the South Atlantic" – Jack Bataldi

This was a terrific talk for this precise time, previewing birds we would see, explaining those we had already seen, all with terrific images. Jack said to be sharp; there would be calls to the bridge for spotting and great camera opportunities. Once again, I took note just of the birds' names to look up later at home, but listened and thoroughly enjoyed the "deeper" explanations by this World Birder. Among the birds – the most impressive, the Albatross – then the Frigate Bird which we would see mostly later in Guanabara Bay in Rio, the Southern Fulmar, Gannets, Petrels, Shearwaters, the Masked Boobies after flying fish in the boat's wake, these in turn after the stirred-up plankton.

After the break I gave my third talk - Religion in Brazil. These notes once again are the "professor's handouts" and the talk only hit the highlights, but my point of departure: you will never really will understand Brazil if you don't understand the religion. The Brazilians themselves claim to be a highly religious people, but it's not always evident!

RELIGION IN BRAZIL. Mike Gaherty "Adventurer" 1972

"Brazil – the world's largest Catholic Country." 150 million believers? A "nominal" Catholicism. About 72 per cent of Brazilians claim Catholicism today as opposed to 90 per -cent in the early 1970s. Why the change?

1. Competition within the church between Progressives and Conservatives
2. Increased competition from Evangelical Protestants like the "Igreja Universal do Reino de Deus." Universal Church of the Kingdom of God and spinoffs.
3. Continuing Afro-Brazilian spiritists
4. Continuing Kardec spiritists
5. Continuing Protestant evangelization from the United States: Assembly of God, "mainline" Protestant churches, Pentecostal churches and Mormons.

HISTORY OF THE CATHOLIC CHURCH IN BRAZIL

1. The prestige of the European Catholic Church during discovery and colonization: they had defeated the Moors and thrown them out of Europe, and with "Royal Patronage," that is, the kings name the clergy, the effective union of Church and State.
2. "Flexible" Portuguese Catholicism: isolation of the church in Brazil, distances, the priests needed a "family" so they made one; concubinage was common and "accepted."
3. Center of colonial life was the plantation with its chapel and not a traditional "parish." The priest was second in charge often on the plantation (as well as being the second son of the owner, the eldest inheriting it all). Part of the power structure. Unmarried daughters often went to the "Convent."
4. Role of the Jesuits. 16th and 17th centuries: missionary work amongst Indians, The "Reductions" or "Jesuit States" in the South near Paraguay ("The Mission" deals with this.) They tried to place

Catholic values on the landholders. But the utopic missions lost out to the "bandeirantes," gold and slave hunters. The Jesuits were expelled for political motives in 1767 from Brazil and Latin America.

5. The Church accepted the concept of Negro slavery.

6. But Catholicism was a "veneer" for the slaves; "real" religion was maintained.

7. 19th Century; Brazil became independent from Portugal and was now an Empire (Dom Pedro I, II). The church was connected to the State, protected as the "official religion," but subordinate to the State. Dom Pedro II who was Catholic and Mason, distanced himself from the Church. The Vatican condemned Masonry, Pedro refused, crisis, some imprisonments and result: separation of church and state in 1889 with the Republic and freedom of religion in Brazil. The Catholic church is weakened.

8. Religion fanaticism in the Northeast. The "Messianic" movements and Sebastianism. Superstition, mysticism, folk religion. Some results.

Lack of priests, immensity of Brazil, little formal contact with Rome.

Even priests in the annual "missions" to reach the people preached that the droughts were a result of sin and that faith, prayer would solve the problems.

Pedra Bonita in Pernambuco State, 1836

Messianic Movement: "Good Jesus" Antônio Conselheiro, War of Canudos 1896

Father Cicero. Juazeiro do Norte, Ceará State. 1880s to 1934. Miracles.

> Friar Damián: fire and damnation and condemnation of the modern Aparecida in Sao Paulo State. 1717 to Present, apparitions of the Virgin.

9. "Renaissance of the Church" in 1920s, 1930s, family and anti-communism.

10. CNBB. National Council of Brazilian Bishops. 1950s, 1960s. Concerns: lack of social justice, in favor of agrarian reform, role of "Dom Hêlder Câmara" - The "Red" bishop: house machine gunned by the para-military right in 1960s, 1970s. "Violence of hunger" Liberation Theology. [I meet him by chance in Recife]. The Catholic "left." Priests murdered; nuns, as well when allied with poor.

11. Reactions of the "right" to President Goulart's "base reforms" of the 1960s. "Tradition, Family and Property" Anti-left, anti-Communist, in favor of military.

12. 1964-1985. Military arrested and tortured leftist Catholics. But the church reacted and became the main force against dictatorship, the only institution that could protest the disappeared and dead without repercussion: the Military did not "dare."

13. The Church today: (see the introduction and concerns, p. 1)

RELIGION: THE OTHER BRAZIL

1. African spiritism: Page estimates 1/3 of Brazilians participate in some way.
   Religious syncretism: "mixture" of religions"
   The "orixás" or saints. Possession by the saint.
   Ritual, mythology, and customs.
   Xangô Recife
   Candomblé Bahia
   (Indian version of same: "Pajelança" in Amazon region)

2. "Macumba," "Umbanda" and "Quimbanda" Rio, São Paulo
Total mixture of Catholic, African, Eastern Mysticism.
"Amorphous" or hard to define, pin down. Reincarnation,
the "spirits" both Catholic and other. Magic may be involved,
hexes in Quimbanda.

3. Kardec Spiritism 1854 and today. Allen Kardec, France.
Spiritism based on the Bible and reinterpreted, reincarnation,
no heaven or hell, The person can better himself, but no going
back. Spiritist healing (Arigó). Chico Xavier – medium and
"spirit" writing.

4. The Evangelicals
Edir Macedo and Universal Church of the Kingdom of God
(Estimated that the Catholic Church loses 600 000 to his
religious "wave" each year.) Use of media on massive scale,
constant services, tithing, no alcohol or drugs. Street corner
evangelizing, promise of economic success, exorcism as basis of
faith. Self-betterment, discipline, hard work. Dynamic.

5. "Believers" "Crentes" and the Northeast
Debates/ old church versus Protestant "invaders"
"The Vulture and the Protestant preacher" Story-poem in the
"Cordel" Sugar cane rum and the Protestants

6. Role of John Paul II and the Catholic "Evangelization"

I don't know if it was the most enjoyed talk of the trip to this point, but
it evoked the most questions, many having to do with what went on at Pai
Edu's just last night. There was discussion and debate amongst adventurers
of the "trance" and / or "slain in the spirit" of our folks. There was also
an opportunity to elucidate on Padre Cícero and his "the host turning into
blood" miracle, and role as a northeastern "messiah." And I really tried to

explain Brazil's "relaxed Catholicism" as opposed to Spain's history. Harry was in the back and had a lot to say about the latter.

The folks might get another chance to be tired of me because Steve wanted the "Introduction to Salvador" talk tomorrow a.m. – the reason: we are to dock in mid-afternoon.

P.M. At Sea

2:00 p.m. Eli gave another terrific talk, this on Bahia, its music and origins. To do this he had to trace slavery in Bahia, the music the slaves brought with them became the origin of Brazil's national dance – the samba – and finally the mélange of nationally popular Brazilian singers from Bahia; there were many. Dorival Caymmi, João Gilberto of Bossa Nova fame, Caetano Veloso and his sister Maria Betania and more. Eli had video clips of it all, including the history of Bahia's Carnival, perhaps second to Rio in national fame, with Oludum the main Carnival "bloco" [samba school] in Bahia. For those keeping score Eli had done the music from the Amazon, from Recife and the Northeast, and now Bahia and the samba, no small accomplishment.

CC: Drinks, lots of conversation, a chance for all staff to mix with adventurers and trade reactions, experiences and questions. Ship videographer Ronaldo Teves (long time AT staffer originally from Hawaii, of Portuguese origin) gave us a 40 minute "preview" of the trip video, in effect almost the first half of the trip. I've forgotten to mention him and his methodology. He corners Captain's crew, AL and AAL and staff for "spontaneous" spots on things seen and visited. I had already done Manaus, Belém, and Recife, the naturalists the on-shore jungle trip, the Belém zoo and important birds, fish and animals. He caught all those "critters" on board and the shrieks, running and capturing of them.

After dinner there was another late p.m. visit to Amy's, we both by now pretty familiar with each other, and I add, glad to see each other. She filled me in on the latest "snafu," Brazilian customs' wanting to inspect the ship at each docking (she thinks an excuse for good drinks and snacks), but an "invitation" not to be turned down. She said she liked being my dance partner and when would she get a chance to teach me "real samba." "Rio, I guess, see if you can get away to join us at the private 'samba' performance at the Scenarium? You know 'gringos' can't dance samba (that's what the Brazilians say) but after two or three of the Scenarium's 'loaded caipirinas' my grandfather could dance samba!" We managed some close time, a kiss or two, that's it.

18

⋯❖⋯

DAY TWO: RECIFE TO SALVADOR

July 14th. 9:00 a.m.

MIKE'S INTRODUCTION TO SALVADOR

SALVADOR DA BAHIA, ITS HISTORY AND IMPORTANCE

Salvador da Bahia, as it is known by the Brazilians, is the 4th largest city in Brazil after Rio, São Paulo and Brasília, a major economic hub of Brazil's Northeast and its most famous tourist site after Rio with its beaches and carnival. Bahia has all the latter and in fact boasts that its carnival is the largest in Brazil, but with an African flavor. This author can attest to its Barra Beach, rated the 3rd best in the world by a European magazine! You will get a chance to agree with me or not!

The city was founded in 1549, became one of the richest "captaincies" during the colonial period and then capital of all Brazil for almost two hundred years until the capital was transferred to Rio in the 19th century. It vies with Rio for its natural attractions and history. It has dozens of miles of pristine white-sand beaches along the Atlantic Coast, one of the most picturesque old city centers of all Brazil (its two-tiered upper and lower cities connected by the famous Lacerda Elevator). There is an entirely separate modern city of skyscrapers and businesses to its north today.

The old city center has the original government buildings from the 16th century, the main plaza, the old Cathedral Plaza with the original Jesuit Church, the most beautiful baroque church in all Brazil, The "São Francisco" church, and the famous "Pelourinho" or Slave Block Plaza nearby. Bahia was the center of Brazil's slave trade for four hundred years, based on sugar cane originally and tobacco of later days. The lower city with its customs' buildings, port and colorful "Mercado Modelo" are just some of the highlights.

Culturally it is still the center of Afro-Brazilian culture in Brazil, its famous carnival, its folk ballet, its many religious rituals of "candomblé" and its folk dance-defense art of "Capoeira" and more. Literary figures from the 16th century to now abound, particularly its most famous writer Jorge Amado. And one of Brazil's best-known religious shrines combining Catholic and African religions, the Church of Bonfim, is just another attraction.

I've probably spent as much time in Salvador, cumulatively, as in Recife and Rio; I wrote about it all in "Adventures" but here are a few highlights:

I was first in Bahia in 1966, here's the gist and some anecdotes:

1. To check out "cordel" situation: Cuíca de Santo Amaro, Rodolfo Cavalcante
2. Most important: to get to know this important Brazilian city, old colonial capital, and "city of mystery" of Jorge Amado; "cordel" would have to wait. The goal was to get to really know Bahia. All through the lens of "Bahia de Todos os Santos" by Jorge Amado.
3. The absolute beauty of the setting: the sea and "orla" - the long beaches on the east, the upper and lower old city. See "Adventures" from 1966.

Investigating Jorge's Bahia …

By day:

Upper city: Government buildings/ Catedral – Praça da Sé/ Terreiro de Jesus/ Igreja de São Francisco/ Old Pelourinho/ Nossa Senhora do Rosário/ Baixa dos Sapateiros/ Funicular/ Igreja de Santa Bárbara/ Praça dos Quinze Mistérios/ and Elevador Lacerda

Lower city: "saveiro" dock, fish Market, Loide Lines, Bahiana Line, and especially the Mercado Modelo with Cordel poets/ Feira de Água dos Meninos/ Igreja do Bonfim - Oxalá

By night:

Capoeira/ some candomblé/ out with friends to clubs/see "City of Mystery," including Jorge Amado's old "Tabaris" Club

Where I bunked: "A Portuguesa" on Avenida 7; dorm near Piedade Plaza; restaurant in the Barra and swimming. The Portuguese Experience

Cf. Pierre Verger, photography/ Jorge Amado, novels/ Castro Alves Poetry

11:00 a.m.

Steve's Plan for On-Shore Salvador

NOON: Early Lunch on Board
Day 1- p.m. and evening
Tour of Upper City, Historic Arca 2 p.m. (option of tomorrow a.m. as well)

Return to the ship for quick rest and shower.
Mercado Modelo plus Dinner on Own 5:30 p.m.
Balé Folclorico da Bahia 9 p.m.

Day 2:
A.M. Swim, snorkel Barra Beach or free to explore. 9:00 a.m.
Lunch on board
Historic Upper City
Igreja do Bonfim
Back on board – "Bahian Dinner." "Adventurer" moves on south to next stop at Ilhéus.

19

IN SALVADOR I

July 14th p.m. We all had the regular lunch and waited for the "all clear" from Captain Tony letting us know we had survived another bout of Brazilian bureaucracy and been "liberated" to begin our time in the city. I was called to the bridge, then dining room to do P.R. and translate for the customs' officials. Much laughter, small-talk and they enjoying Chef Reynaldo's hospitality. That may have helped us get off on time for the rest of that big day.

I was assigned to one group of adventurers for the first activity, a walk to the Lacerda Elevator, up to the main government plaza and then the "Old City Tour." Harry a veteran and Buck were assigned to the other groups, but we all had local guides. There was always great rapport but a potentially sensitive situation – when their English was not up to snuff and that was common, I gently had to graciously, humorously and with great tact volunteer to "help them clarify" something. Most of the time it went well. Adventurers were warned this would be a long walking day, not up-hill strenuous, but very warm and humid, to be sure and take their ship water bottles, some Brazilian money (in small bills; they had an agent on board just after we docked for money changing) and, later after a ship break and shower, credit cards for some larger purchases at the Modelo Market.

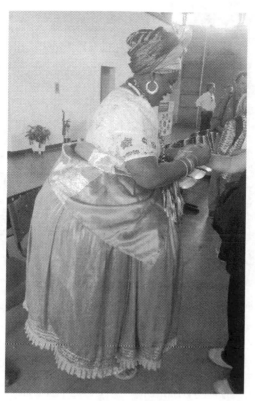

Bahiana and Lucky Bracelets, Salvador

After disembarking from "Adventurer" we walked along the cobblestone dock, inside a just barely air-conditioned terminal where we were greeted by the very large size (on purpose) Bahian ladies in their "candomblé" outfits of turbans, embroidered blouses, huge billowing skirts and an excess of necklaces and bangles on their wrists. They tied the "Welcome to Bahia" ribbons on our wrists (you are not supposed to cut them off; let them finally wear off for good luck), showed us the door – literally – to where we walked back 400 years to a crowded, hot, humid, tropical lower city of Salvador. We were directed to the iconic landmark the Lacerda Elevator where we joined the real Bahians of all colors and ages in the small elevator cabin (once again, no real air conditioning, but yes air moving; why not say it? Body odor in the tropics!). The ride was swift, a little like a New York skyscraper to the top where we walked out into the main government plaza of old Bahia.

Salvador, the Elevator and Lower City

There was a flurry of sights in the upper city that morning from the Tomé de Souza statue of the 16th century founder of Bahia, the walk along the street with "capoeira" artists, mimes, the beautiful view from the street's edge to the wall overlooking the lower city, the Mercado, the docks and the "Reconcavo" or big bay and its ocean-going ships. We walked by the renowned Medical School of Bahia. I chimed in, not our guide, telling of seeing the severed heads of Lampião, Maria Bonita and Curisco, Brazil's most famous bandits, all caught in a police showdown after years of pursuit, heads cut off and put in kerosene cans for a macabre odyssey through the towns of the backlands to prove to the people they were really dead. That was 1938. The heads were only removed after a wave of protest in the late 1960s. They were in yellowed jars of formaldehyde when I saw them, objects of study by scientists of Determinism to see what makes bandits tick! Such scientists, predecessors of racism of the times were the villains in Jorge Amado's wonderful thesis novel "The Miracle Shop" ["Tenda dos Milagres"].

We walked by the Cathedral, the old Jesuit Church with the Jesuit father still in mass stole and chasuble far above, through a plaza with Bahiana ladies in their small food stands offering the popular spicy local food and snacks to the locals and the tourists. Some adventurers insisted on trying them – "abaré, acarajé" and the rest.

Patio of the Church of São Francisco

Then we all proceeded down a narrow plaza called the "Terreiro de Jesus" to the most famous church in Brazil, São Francisco and its baroque splendor. The Jesuits came with the first discoverers and colonizers but were soon followed by the Franciscans.

The Baroque Interior

The latter built this magnificent edifice in 1708-1723; the interior nave, main altar and a series of side altars are literally covered in minute wood carving with gold gilt on it. Adventurers, no rookies to churches throughout the world, were astonished; second to the gold gilt were the largest, most ornate panels of Portuguese blue tiles up to that time in Brazil, in the church itself and in its surrounding interior patio.

Lascivious Angels, São Francisco Church

I have to apologize for perhaps a thought bordering on "sacrilege" – Jorge Amado in his famous "Dona Flor and Her Two Husbands" has his roguish hero Vadinho going to the church to hit up the pastor for a loan and then remarking on the lasciviousness of the hundreds of baroque, well – endowed angels therein. One of the men in our group did comment to me after seeing them that he understood that even Franciscans had to get their kicks! No comment.

Oludum Girl, Salvador

I talked to one of the remaining monks, there are few, in the atrium and he lamented the lack of vocations for the priesthood today, the general "secularism" of the world and the horrendous din of noise from the Bahian "samba school" Oludum with its center nearby. "The drums go on all night long. You can't sleep, much less pray." At the same time, he did admit that it was tourism and donations that keep the church open today.

Since the area outside is loaded with tourist shops, adventurers were given just twenty minutes to peruse the same. In that same busy plaza in front of the São Francisco I ran into, by accident, an important part of Brazilian Culture – a shop dedicated to Brazilian Kardec Spiritism and its most important "Vidente" or "Seer" Chico Xavier (1910 to 2002). There was no time to alert adventurers who were scattered in the area shopping or sightseeing, and my time in the shop was perhaps a total of three minutes when I snapped a photo of two or three of his book covers, rushing on the way to the Pelourinho Plaza. It is important to fill in the gaps here, even if just for another minute. Chico from Minas Gerais (as his cohort

Spiritualist healer Arigó) was a Kardec Spiritualist, but one of a kind, he was a "médium" (one who could communicate with spirits) who "saw" writings of the spirits and "wrote" no less than 450 books and thousands of letters using a process called "psychography." He is credited with 50 million books sold. It is of interest that he called his spiritual guide Emmanuel who lived in ancient Rome as Publius Lentulus, was later reincarnated as a priest in Spain and then a professor at the Sorbonne! Chico Xavier channeled diverse spirits and claimed he could write nothing unless they communicated and cooperated. This is just one more aspect of religion in Brazil, not a small one.

We were all herded just a few blocks from the church, walking carefully on the centuries' old cobblestones, past the Third Order Franciscan Church next to the big one, with its intricate Baroque carved stone façade. Farther down the street is the most famous plaza in all Brazil — the Pelourinho — or Slave Block. It is no secret Salvador is the "blackest" city in Brazil, the major site of importation of slaves from Africa from the 16th century to 1888 when it all ended. This plaza was where the slaves were brought in chains from the slave ships and auctioned to prospective owners — the sugar cane and tobacco plantation owners called "Coroneis" [Colonels — an honorary military title]. The pillar ["pelourinho"] itself is long gone, but not its memory. Down a steep incline is yet another church, "A Igreja de Nossa Senhora dos Pretos" or the black brotherhood church built and designed for Black Brazilians.

Also in that same plaza was one of the most important places in all Brazil for my research — A Casa de Jorge Amado — the research center, museum and bookstore dedicated to Brazil's most famous writer. He was important in my dissertation and my favorite Brazilian writer — more to come. There were just ten minutes for adventurers to go into the lobby on the first floor and see the bookstore. Several hurriedly bought novels recommended by me; everything he wrote is in English translation. I would be talking much more about him in just another day when "Adventurer" moved on to his home town of Ilhéus in southern Bahia State.

We all retraced our way up the hill back to the main plaza, the street and the Lacerda Elevator – this time many stopped to take probably the best view picture of Bahia's Bay from the side of the elevator. Then we had that "folkloric" experience of being whisked down to the lower city and the short walk back to the ship for showers and a snack.

At 5:00 p.m. most of the group left the ship again and did the short two block walk to the "Mercado Modelo" [Model Market] still the center of tourism in Salvador with a restaurant on the third floor where adventurers could get real Bahian food, the famous Afro-Brazilian dishes. The market had a lot of "bugigangas" or "stuff," but also some quality items in clothes and embroidery and a very nice gem shop on the third floor (many of the mines for semi-precious stones in Brazil are in Bahia). Some headed directly for the latter. The city licenses and keeps an eye on the shops so all stones are "legitimate." Out in front now in 1972 is a kind of "hippy fair" with homemade and costume jewelry but at very reasonable prices. And we lucked out – it was early enough that the "cordel" poetry stand of one of the best-known poets, a person in my dissertation, was still there selling his goods, I mean Rodolfo Coelho Cavalcante. Some adventurers had heard enough of all that to be interested so when I mentioned it, we all went out to meet the poet. He was surprised, even astonished to see me in such company, and when I explained I was giving lectures on the International Adventurer Expedition Ship his eyes lit up, maybe with $ signs. I asked Rodolfo to declaim one of his poems and we decided on "The Man on the Moon," his version of the 1969 famous landing. He would declaim (he was a pro at that) and I would translate, all a big success. More of a success was that many adventurers bought copies, many copies, included as gifts and souvenirs for back home. Rodolfo was full of himself as usual and told everyone I was his "biographer," a bit of an exaggeration.

People had lots of time for an early dinner at Camaféu de Oxossi's Restaurant in the market with the all Bahian menu, and I had time to get away to the bar for twenty minutes with Rodolfo and Camaféu (a black man, minor character in several of Jorge Amado's novels about Salvador) who traded anecdotes, boasts and maybe lies trying to top each other in impressing me. Rodolfo was still into his beers, but was tickled to see me; he did mention a visit to the ship and a poetry performance, but was disappointed when I told him there was just no time on the busy schedule. With my fragile stomach I had to very carefully and graciously turn down Camaféu's offer for dinner but did accept a terrific shrimp cocktail along with the cold beer. He was pleased we brought in all the customers.

Another reason for dinner at Camaféus's place was the terrific view to the bay, the old fish market to the side, the ocean going ships but especially the local sailing-cargo boats with one sail (made famous in Amado's novels, heroically saving passengers on a sinking ocean liner in the Bay during a storm – the "Saveiros"). Many times later on the trip adventurers would thank me and the IA for this experience when they really felt like they were in Brazil, with Brazilians and eating real Brazilian food.

One casualty - Lady Grouch   tripped on the stairs going up to the restaurant and I had to get her to the nearest "Pronto Socorro"[First Aid Station] where they taped up her ankle, sold her a crutch, and Buck offered to get her back to the ship, she complaining all the way and threatening to sue every Brazilian in sight.

Iemanjá, Goddess of the Sea

Capoeira at Its Best

We all hustled out of the Market at about 8:00 p.m., did the 10-minute walk to the ship, freshened up and were ready for the great new adventure that night – the Folkloric Ballet of Bahia. We loaded into vans at 8:30 and parked in the only close by place, the small plaza at the bottom of the Pelourinho called the Baixa dos Sapateiros. We had warned adventurers that there would be up hill walking, at times over cobblestones, and lots and lots of steps and stairways. What I did not like was there were some dark areas, in fact I'm not sure I would have found my way through in daylight. We were told later that it is a favorite mugger's run at the tourists. Easy enough to know now. The show was terrific, highly professional and I understand they tour the world, beautiful costumes. Having a lot of experience with Bahian folklore the months I spent in this city and the folklorists I actually knew, I can say its main virtue was its authenticity. Carefully choreographed with the exact steps and nuances of movement of the candomblé rituals (we did not attend one of those but this was just as good), it featured the goddess of the sea Iemanjá, Doña Bárbara and Oxossi. Local dances harking back to the sugar cane fields, Maculêlê (sticks in rhythm) and some of the best "Capoeira" I had seen in Brazil.

We asked for two police escorts on the way back, one in front, one in the rear and that probably saved our butts. Everyone was tired, needed a cool shower and rest for a very busy next day. I forgot, before the show once again the theater offered each adventurer a wonderful "caipirinha" – icy cold, right amount of "cachaça," sugar, and lime. Hmmm good. And if you wanted a second, so be it. Put everyone in a jovial mood for the show.

Amy was in the office on the ship land line when we walked in. I walked over, said hi and she just waved and indicated "Can't talk now." I would catch her tomorrow evening at CC. Grouchy Lady was feeling better after a couple of scotches in her room and had decided it was not Camaféu's fault she had slipped. Whew!

20

"YANKEE, GO HOME!"

July 15th. We were awakened by Steve for the days' activities, but with one unexpected bit of news – "Adventurer" was the victim during the night of a Brazilian habit and custom – the ship was hit by the graffiti people. Graffiti is all over any available city wall. There are plenty of guards and night watchmen; the culprits must have come quietly in the water and then sprayed the ship. Bright red "Yankee Go Home," not original but getting everyone's attention, particularly Captain Tony. He was steaming! (There were some choice comments about the lazy Brazilians and how they never learned anything from their discovers and colonizers, meaning we Portuguese,) I would be delayed for one hour to join the morning tour due to translation duty with the customs' officials, the dock police and an unexpected surprise, the **DOPS** agent of 1967 days! (I think maybe he just wanted to see "Adventurer" as well.) Sérgio back then was worried about my research "on that commie Jorge Amado" and the "commie" Literature professor I interviewed at the University of Bahia.

The paint turned out to be cleanable and a crew would have it off and any touchup repainting of the hull by our departure tonight. Customs were all very apologetic for the "inconvenience." Sérgio however did have some words and advice for me. He said Odálio his **DOPS** colleague had informed **DOPS** he met me in Manaus and was in touch and a little pissed off he did not get to see the ship, so he, Sérgio, thought he would take us up on the "invitation." He laughed, saying Odálio would really be pissed off at that. I, with permission of Captain Tony, and being assured DOPS needed to be involved after the spray painting, gave Sérgio the quick tour and that good coffee and snacks outside the dining room. He was fully apprised of all my activities and the "Letters" books and smiled and called me "Arretado" a time or two in the talk. He didn't really have anything new to report, noting the government was continuing its due diligence and vigilance of the Left (including Chico Buarque) while accomplishing "great things" for Brazil. We parted with an "abraço;" he was reassured I was doing cultural duties and no research, but ended with a not so veiled warning to "not do anything stupid."

Porto da Barra Beach

I took a taxi to Barra beach and adventurers were all frolicking in those great gentle waves; it took just a jiffy to join them. A French tourism magazine did a spread on Salvador, its white sand dunes to the north and all its exotic offerings, but waxed euphoric on Barra Beach as "The Third Best Beach in the World." I won't go there. Suffice to say for two months in November and December of 1966 I and my Peace Corps buddy Don swam at the beach each a.m. before a wonderful lunch at our Portuguese Boarding House Restaurant on a small peninsula directly off the beach. I was out on a limb again since I had recommended it to AT for this trip, but they researched it, found it okay, so we did it. Now in 1972 every beach in tourist Brazil has a cadre of police with belly clubs patrolling, Barra among them. It's very small, in a perfect crescent next to the old Portuguese Fort and just down the way from Salvador's best light house where the long, straight sandy beaches will run for no less than twenty miles to the north.

Adventurers had arrived at 9:30 in the vans; beach boys ran up with rental chairs and the like. The beach would be crowded in another hour, a favorite of the middle and upper class neighborhood surrounding it and for tourists from the many hotels in the neighborhood. It was not what you wanted if you wanted to be alone, but it was a true Brazilian beach going experience. The was beautiful turquoisc-blue water, cool when you got in, but not cold at all, with only slight waves from the huge bay. Fishing boats, kayaks and the like were moored off one end, but did not interfere with the swimming. There was not really room for soccer games, but the Brazilians liked to play "frescobol," batting a tennis ball back and forth, and a volleyball net or two were up. It was the swimming, the gentle sun early in the day and light brown-white sand, plus beautiful girls now in bikinis and what looked like body builders in their "sungas." After my late arrival I still had about an hour to swim and then we all were back in the vans to the ship. Several people wanted to know about the spray painting and what happened; I just told them it was resolved; we were far from the only targets in Brazil and would be ready to roll this evening.

Whew. After lunch there was one final outing to cap off the Salvador experience and something new for everyone. We did the long drive through traffic to the Igreja do Bonfim on the Itapagipe Peninsula south of the old city center. This is yet another of Bahia's famous churches but for distinct reasons.

The Miracle Room, Bonfim Church

Candomblé Figures, Salvador

Built in the 1770s it housed the image of the crucified Jesus (from Setubal in Portugal) and over the years became known for its miracles attributed to Jesus, thus one of its main features is the "miracle room" where plastic body parts – heads, hands, legs and such – hang from the ceiling, "memories" or "ex-votos" acknowledging miraculous cures (they were of Plaster of Paris in my visit in 1966). A second and no less important reason for the church's fame is its syncretism of Catholic and Afro-Brazilian religions. On the feast day in January dozens of the ladies of the "candomblé" rite process for the eight kilometers from Salvador's lower city and its first church of "Conceição da Praia," the ladies in all their finery. Once arriving at Bonfim on the Itapagipe Peninsula they proceed to wash the outside steps of the church and lay flowers in homage singing praises in Yoruba (or Nagô) the African slave language associated with "candomblé" in honor of Oxalá or Jesus. They then join the Catholic rituals inside the church. Bonfim is one of a half dozen major pilgrimage sites in all Brazil and the "festa" attracts hundreds of thousands throughout the year.

The visit to Bonfim with IA was my first since 1966, and along with staff duties I indeed did my own pilgrimage, including an impulsive moment which I kissed the cross of Jesus, the patron saint, at an exposition of the Blessed Sacrament with Christ on the Crucifix (but with no time to formulate a proper prayer request). For our guests, first-timers to Brazil, this was a magnificent lesson in Brazilian culture and folk-popular religions. The "miracle room" or "promises room" with today's plastic arms, legs, hands, heads of humans – the "Ex-votos" – was a revelation to all. As usual, the unexpected came up: an "emergency" trip to the gift shop where there was a small bathroom for a desperate lady adventurer. There was a lot of hurried up Portuguese! But it had its reward: she was grateful, and I saw all the stuff they sell to people who come. Bonfim is as major place, glad I was there again.

Everyone was pretty well tired from the intensive two days and ready for our refuge – the air-conditioned comfort of "Adventurer." At CC that afternoon Steve prepped them for the big day in Ilhéus tomorrow. We would be in early in the a.m. have time to do Customs again and be off at 9:00 for a big day, for history, for culture, and now again for the naturalists. Steve asked me to give a short, very short, introduction to Jorge Amado for what we would see tomorrow. Here's the abbreviated version:

BAHIA THROUGH THE LENS OF JORGE AMADO. Mike Gaherty

Placing Jorge Amado:

  a. He was one of the "romancistas do Nordeste" along with Raquel de Queiróz, José Lins do Rego and Graciliano Ramos.
  b. He was a contemporary of Colombia's García Marquez and Peru's Mário Vargas Llosa. They won the Nobel; he did not. He also wrote at the time of Carlos Fuentes, a famous Mexican novelist.
  c. A Best Seller in Brazil; it's bestselling novelist and best known until his death.
  d. He was the heart and soul of Bahia, my "guide" to that part of Brazil.
4. Famous novels: "Mar Morto," Jubiabá," "Tenda dos Milagres", "Dona Flor e seus Dois Mariodos", "Gabriela Cravo e Canela" (we shall see the scene in Ilhéus).

Dinner was enjoyable, I ordered from the menu, steak, baked potato and salad, this because of a slight upset, maybe from Camaféu's shrimp cocktail. I was not alone; several guests said they loved the Bahian food, "going down."

21

ILHÉUS – CHILDHOOD HOME OF JORGE AMADO PLUS SOME BIRDS

July 16th. I ate breakfast with the fellow who designed the thrusters for the Apollo Space Program. He liked our talk of Captain Video, an early black and white TV "space show" of the 1950s, and Werner von Braun's lectures on the plan to go to the moon on Disney's "Wide World of Color." He quoted Von Braun: "I aimed for the stars, but I hit London." We talked of "The Right Stuff" and Apollo 13 suspense.

ILHÉUS

Ilhéus is a large city in southern Bahia State noted for its rich agriculture of tobacco, sugar cane but especially the cacao plantations. Bahia will produce along with Rio Grande do Sul in southern Brazil the best chocolate in all Brazil. And cigar lovers hanker for those stogies. It is a relatively recent phenomenon in the Brazilian economic story, its heyday being the early 20th century when there were land wars and many deaths in the battles for control of the rich lands. There was a wild and wooly "frontier" atmosphere with gun toting bad guys and bodyguards and mercenary fighters for the "Colonels" or rich landowners vying for control and dough. Jorge Amado, Brazil's most famous writer, was born and raised on one of the cacao plantations and wrote early novels of the area's history and strife, the first in stark realism with a Marxist flavor, but later (after Amado learned of Stalin's Gulag and reneged on his Marxist affiliation) delightful, humorous, colorful and entertaining novels of the area, the famous "Gabriela Clove and Cinnamon" being the best. IA will visit the family mansion in Ilhéus and later the famous brothel now nightclub and the Vesúvio Bar where the main characters of Nacib and Gabriela live out the story.

The visit to a working cacao plantation and the rich natural habitat (the naturalists had a field day with the birding) were an additional highlight, a terrific addition to the Expedition.

ILHÉUS - THE EXCURSION

We arrived on Nossa Senhora da Aparecida saint's day; she is the equivalent in Brazil to France's Lourdes and Portugal's Fatima. On this the major religious festival day in Brazil, the church was closed. Hmm. The excursion passed by Jorge Amado's father's house, now the Amado museum. It was closed when our group went by, but others who caught it were impressed by the old manual typewriter Jorge used to write all the novels. Next door was something more important: I ran quickly into the Vesúvio Bar (the scene of much of Jorge Amado's novel, "Gabriela, Clove and Cinnamon"), took photos, not realizing we would return later in the day. This day merits many photos.

Gabriela, Nacib, Ilhéus

We walked by a tourist shop with the cute clerk standing by the "kitsch" character of Gabriela. Nacib her lover and some-time husband and bar owner is on the shelf to the right. Another thing the adventurers were "thirsting for" was the chance to buy Brazilian souvenirs. Fortunately, on the way to the bus we stopped at a chocolate shop (one of Bahia's best products) and directed the entire crowd inside. Never was there such a good sales day for the store. One adventurer bought miniature Bahian chocolates for his entire staff of employees, saying it was perfect! One of the finer local delicacies in Brazil is the local liqueur ["licor"] made from an unending variety of fruits, but also of chocolate. Free samples were provided, and many bottles of that good stuff were jammed into homeward luggage (if not imbibed in adventurer rooms).

The bus took us to the cacao plantation, 40 kilometers outside Ilhéus and it was a very pleasant surprise. There is once again the already mentioned Jorge Amado connection. He grew up on his parents' cacao plantation near Ilhéus and was witness to or heard from relatives of the famous local battles for land and riches. Once again, there are several books: the original "Cacau," "Terras do Sem Fim" but the modern delight

"Gabriela, Clove and Cinnamon" tells the story in spectacular fashion in the era of the 1920s.

We all were taken to the cacao grove, saw the large orangish – yellow fruits; the guide cut one open and we saw the dozens of white cacao "seeds" inside. It was these that would be dried in the sun and eventually ground into a paste to make cacao and then chocolate! They showed us a long drying rack where a fellow raked the seeds, turning them over in the sun to dry.

Next was the much-anticipated walking tour through the forest led by the naturalists. Since I was always assigned to culture, here was a rare chance to see some of the Brazil I had never seen. There was a small glitch when I missed my assigned walking tour, but for a good reason. It turns out someone must "bring up the rear" and keep track of those adventurers perhaps with walking aids or a recent hip or knee replacement, such was my duty of helping one of the elderly adventurers back to the bus. I managed after getting her safely to her seat to do a hike alone when I saw blue Morpho butterflies, armadillo holes, cutter ants, cattle herons, the river and several colorful birds. (I believe there was some criticism for my not staying with the group, but taking care of the lady with her cane prevented this; by the time I got her to the bus, the tour had gone on far ahead. In fact, I walked into the forest and did not see them, so it was not my fault). For me, this place had the potential for the best yet for Brazilian nature. The problem was without the naturalists I missed seeing many birds I heard and wouldn't know the name of them if I did see them.

There was a start and a scare however. While walking through dense forest on a narrow and very wet path I heard a rustle and then a loud grunt and a creature went slamming across the trail in front of me. It scared the you know what out of me. It happened so quickly I didn't get any pictures, but did see it clearly and am sure that indeed it was a tapir. Buck told me later that we were just on the fringe of tapir territory, but with all the forest and water, including the beautiful river running through the plantation, I had lucked out.

Lunch was served to a thirsty, hot and famished crowd: rice, chicken, beef, beans, flan, cafezinho, real Brazilian food! And icy beer, very welcomed by all the guests. Later there was time to walk through the "fazenda" house, super elegant and reflecting the wealth of the cacao plantation owners.

The naturalists had a field day, maybe a record breaker; we would hear all about it at CC, but there was more to come.

Candomblé Dress, Tarot, Búzios, Ilhéus Shop

Back in town we drove to a small "folk art" market. They sold Bahian Carnival costume "accouterments" including the "kitsch" men's and women's sex organs! Such items were the props for Vadinho and gang during carnival in Bahia in the movie "Dona Flor" based on yet another Amado novel. This was indeed a surprise to me and something, modesty or whatever, prevented me from pointing out such items to the guests. And there on sale were some story-poems of "cordel!" I for sure did not want the "cordel" to be connected or related in any way to the Carnival sex costumes, the proximity misconstrued or misunderstood. I'm getting defensive – no relation whatsoever. The shop also had tarot cards and beautiful "candomblé" dresses.

We returned to the Vesúvio Bar, a highlight for me. This was the main scene, made fiction, in Jorge Amado's "Gabriela Clove and Cinnamon." There were cold beers with naturalists and photographers Kelly and Jack and we saw the amazing arrival of the parakeet flight in the plaza at 5 p.m. There were hundreds if not thousands and they made a raucous din for about an hour before sunset.

I got to talk to one of my favorite guests, he from Brooklyn and the Bronx; he grew up amidst all the falderal of life on 42 St. in New York! For the Nebraska farm boy this was a spicy story. And someone did me the favor of taking a picture of me with the Plaster of Paris "kitsch" statue of Jorge "seated" at a bench in front of the bar. I haven't said yet that there were beautiful larger than life title scenes of Gabriela and Nacib inside the bar on its walls.

Most everyone had at least two "caipirinhas" so the vans were loud with chit-chat on our twenty-minute return ride to the ship. It was time for the naturalists to shine with reports of all the birds, a hurried up shot of a tapir by Buck. But his main story, he said one of the highlights of his life, took place on one of the options for Ilhéus; going the other direction was the Eco-Parque de Una. A full to capacity van took adventurers there while most of us did the cacao plantation and Ilhéus. I think it ended a draw with one big moment for the Una crowd – they had a fleeting glance at a wild Golden Headed Lion Tamarin (we would see a reserve outside of Rio) while walking a 30-meter-high suspension bridge over the reserve. And Willie got shots of several fishy creatures in the nearby Maruim River.

Songbird, Cacau Plantation, Ilhéus

But the cacao plantation naturalists saw the birds! I think I saw one or two they even missed! Cattle egrets were, well, with the cattle; the birders had images transferred from cameras of a "Corrupião," looking like a Baltimore Oriole, Martins, a "Masked Water Tyrant," a "Grey Hooded Atila," a beautiful Kinglet Manakin with a red top (I may have seen) and maybe three dozen others. I watched and followed the Masked Water Tyrant feeding in the lush grass and another exotic bird feeding on seeds on rocks in the beautiful clear river and most amazing for me, first time, long lines of leaf cutter ants. I must have watched for 20 minutes.

Dinner was with a couple from Texas, long – time AT adventurers but with a surprise, the wife had read a lot of the "new wave" novelists from Latin America including Borges from Argentina, Vargas Llosa from Peru, García Márquez from Colombia, Carlos Fuentes from Mexico, and her favorite, Jorge Amado! I asked why and she had a succinct answer, "A Master's in Spanish and Portuguese – Spanish American and Brazilian Literature" from Austin. We immediately launched into conversation in Portuguese, but just a bit, the others at table did not know it. But we would get together at CC two or three times on the trip and speak. In the meantime, she thanked me profusely for all the talk on Jorge Amado and we laughed a lot reminiscing over "Gabriela, Clove and Cinnamon." She said my talks "Were the best and what's next?" I said I wasn't sure, but there would be an Introduction to Rio and a recounting of escapades with Chico Buarque. I hoped to do one talk just on "cordel" and to end with a two – part overview of Brazil, down the way.

As a matter of fact Steve had talked to me and we decided to show one of the glitzsy commercial movies based on Amado novels that night – a "goodbye" to Bahia, Ilhéus and Jorge, but a big risk because Jorge has no end of steamy sex scenes and the Barreto Brothers wanted it all in the film. I would have to be present to introduce the film and answer any questions later (and anticipate objections). I had already thought of a defense – "We are in Brazil, it's their culture and their way of life and that's why we're here, to experience it." I did do a disclaimer before about the sex – how can you miss with Marcelo Mastroianni (for the girls) and Sônia Braga for the guys! That was a good thing to do, probably saved us some grief. I heard later that all the young naturalists saw it in one of their rooms with a bottle of Bacardi, cold Coca Cola and limes and ice. By the way Amy was present, saying she had done both the novel and the movie in Brazil and wouldn't miss it! And she invited me to her room afterwards for "an appropriate discussion."

I told Amy I was embarrassed to show it in classes at U. of N. and honestly, here too, but I and Brazil could not deny Jorge Amado! She said we should have a "hot date" in her room tomorrow night and see "Dona Flor and Her Two Husbands" and laughed! Either way it's Sônia Braga, but with that Brazilian "hunk" José Wilker. We made a tentative "date" for tomorrow night.

22

DID YOU SAY "WHALES"?

July 17th. For me the next two days were a welcome rest, "at sea" and the birders and oceanographic people would keep us all agog with the sea birds and whales of Abrolhos. It was 800 miles from Ilhéus to Rio and with the stop in Abrolhos to whale watch it would take two full days, the morning of the second with my "Introduction to Rio" and Eli's big talk on samba, Carnival in Rio and Carioca music. Incidentally after a chat with Steve I made a special request for one evening off the ship and "off duty" to attend to some private matters in Rio, a "getaway" for me. Chico Buarque and Cristina Maria were on my mind.

As we made our way south toward the "nursery" area for humpback whales coming from the Antarctic for the calving in warmer waters, I admit to a bit of sadness. In effect my Brazilian expertise was 2/3 done, even though the Amazon was not in the same category as the Northeast with Recife and Bahia the old haunts. I guess I was also saying goodbye to all the years of study of Jorge Amado and terrific times in Salvador. On the other hand, Rio de Janeiro awaited and that, in its totality of my research time and energy, almost matched the Northeast. And Steve assured me there would be time on down the coast at sea for the "Universe of Cordel" talk and the last "Overview of Brazil." It had all seemed to go so fast. Steve assured me good times were to come and the "Adventurer" needed Mick Gaherty's knowledge and humor. He also said to relax a bit and let the naturalists be in charge; they were chomping at the bit for what was to come. More on that tomorrow p.m. with the "Intro to Rio."

We were fortunate; the sea was rolling but not too much; there was brilliant blue sky and the water a deep blue. Steve was on his "turf" and Willie too, he having "swum with the whales" all over the planet, including similar nursing grounds off Maui in Hawaii. There was a large photo on one of the stairway walls with a person in full scuba outfit and a huge humpback in front of him; turns out it was Willie. Willie was out on the bow with binoculars, Steve up above with Captain Tony.

Mama Whale Up Close

Almost like clockwork, there they were! Up higher from the bridge, Steve saw the spouts, waved down to Willie who got ready as well. As we came upon them the spouts increased and then suddenly a huge humpback whale breached in front of us. Ooh and aahs. All the adventurers were in all the available viewing space on the bow and the "balcony" below the bridge with their super-duper cameras which I learned act as high-powered binoculars as well. Then another! It turned out to be two pods with three females and calves in one, two and calves in another, so we had, pardon me, a "plethora" of whales. I had never seen anything like it and this was when I needed a better camera and how to use it. You wait for the damned whale to come up and guess where it is going to come up, and if you're lucky, bam! After awhile I just relaxed, Steve saying the videographer and the naturalists would have video film of it all for us to see later. Captain Tony was using "Adventurer" like a motor boat, turning with the whales as they moved, circling around them, meeting them again. He was in no hurry and was excited himself declaring this moment one of his best and that there have been many!

We got to see the amazing sight of calves swimming alongside their mammas and playing! The calves began breaching as well. It became a show to maybe outdo the others. An incredible show. I think we watched for over an hour when the Captain said we must move on. The whales now were much farther off; you could still see spouts but the show was over. I heard no complaints but just those "oohs" and "aahs." Amy sidled up to me, saying "You can't see this in Nebraska young fella!" She was happy for me and for AT and IA. "This really helps for customer satisfaction. We advertised the whales in the brochure, but it's never a guarantee."

That afternoon at CC the naturalists had gotten together with videographer Ronaldo and we saw spectacular video footage of the whole thing. AT provides the adventurers with a video (for a price) at the end of the trip and this would be a great moment. I mentioned earlier the impromptu video interviews with staff at various places on the trip; they would be there too. What a thrill, almost better than seeing it originally. It happened so fast and you try to "imprint" it on your mind to savor later. I wouldn't see my slides until after the trip but didn't expect much. I got tired of trying to prop the camera in front of my eyes and wait for the whales to come up, but probably lucked out for two or three shots.

Dinner was animated and this landlubber just tried to blend in. Most all the adventurers had seen whales time and time again but were happy for this time and praised the experience. But, hey it was over; they wanted to know what we had cooked up for Rio. I said I would let them know tomorrow. But an impromptu unscheduled talk took place in the lounge at 7:00. I'll call it the Willie Show. He talked of all the types of whales one can see on the oceans of the world and had personal images and footage of some of his best experiences – Orcas in the Arctic and Antarctic, Humpbacks off Hawaii, Right Whales, Bruges Whales, and others I'd have to look up. And he had that incredible footage of him "swimming with the whales" in full scuba gear. The bar was open and most adventurers attended because Willie never failed to surprise or entertain.

Entertain. Hmm. A hard act to follow, but Eli and I would take center stage tomorrow with my regular talk on Rio, Eli's "samba" and "carnival" show and Steve's outline for three full days in what we call "A Cidade Maravilhosa" ["The Marvillous City"]. I had to get back to final prep and review for all that but managed to make that "date" with Amy first.

She had been with AT long enough that she had many opportunities for whale watching but was glad for me and the people on board. She had talked to Steve and was more interested in a personal matter – why I had asked for "leave" for an evening, a bit unusual for staffers? I explained in this case, being responsible for much of what would go on and being with adventurers for those three days, I wasn't about to shirk my duties but wanted to see Chico Buarque if I could. A light bulb went on then - what if I convinced him to come aboard for a dinner, an impromptu music session in the lounge with just me and his guitarist and drummer? A shot in the dark to be sure but great publicity for AT, maybe a hoot for him and a thrill for all of us. Was there any "slush fund" to pay for it, maybe $500 USD? And Chico liked "cachaça," maybe the IA barman could arrange a bit of that for some nice "caipirinhas." Amy hesitated, but knowing of the tremendous publicity of anything with Chico, said she would talk to Steve, and yes, the dollars could appear. And there were a couple of nice cabins if Chico and friends wanted to stay on board for breakfast, a ship tour and get off at Parati. Wow! This was one big piece of pie in the sky – but who knows? We made arrangements for me to call Chico from the ship tomorrow night, mc set up our encounter and see what might happen. Makes my head spin.

Amy poured us drinks, that good scotch again, sat down next to me on the divan and we greeted each other properly with one of those kisses. Hmm. After the first drink and she pouring the second she said, "I'm curious. Is it only Chico in Rio? The e-books got here; I've read the "Letters" series now, and I can count four, I think, four hot Carioca women you might want to see. I'll make you a deal – if you postpone that for a later time, [quem sabe quando], maybe I can make it up to you, make it worth your while if you see what I mean. I'm planning on Ipanema so we could do that together anyway. Mike, like I said back, where was it? Manaus? This is all fortuitous, I mean you and me. What do you say?"

"Amy, you've already been amazingly kind even considering anything with Chico. I had thought of maybe seeing a female friend or two, but one for sure would be purely social and catching up, and the three others, well, under the circumstances, they can wait. I don't want to go into it but if you read "Letters II and III" you've got a good idea of what I'm saying. And Amy, I can tell you sincerely, I'd rather be with you."

That was how we left it; a whole lot would be determined by the call to Chico and the outside chance he was free of commitments and willing. We'll know tomorrow night. I'll call using Amy's line from the ship and hope to see him and Marieta the next night, the first in Rio.

23

<hr />

PREPPING FOR THE "MARVILLOUS CITY"

July 18th. Last day at sea before Rio. Steve still wanting adventurers to have a respite from Salvador and to rest up before Rio scheduled just the two big talks today, mine on Rio and Eli's on "Samba" "Carnival" and "Brazilian Popular Music." Unhappily it would be his last; he would be getting off after Rio to head over to Madrid for a commitment – the International Music Festival. (Amy and I had clued him into the possible Chico Buarque "gig on board" and he was all in! He said he even could come up with maybe $200 from his TV show to add to the pot).

9:00 a.m.

MIKE'S TALK ON RIO DE JANEIRO

This entire hour and one half was full of anecdotes, stories and jokes and good times in Rio in 1966 and 1967 doing dissertation research and back in 1969, noting it was all in "Adventures of a 'Gringo' Researcher in Brazil in the 1960s." In the midst of it I gave a short historic overview of Rio:

Notes on History of Rio de Janeiro -More than you need to know!

1. The French enter the Bay of Guanabara in 1555. The Portuguese fight to throw them out from 1565 to 1567. During the battle Portuguese General Mem de Sá (of Salvador fame) was killed.
2. Bahia was still the "seat" of Brazil's "capitanias" and became Brazil's first capital in 1660.
3. In the 18th century (1700s) gold was discovered in Minas Gerais. There was European migration to Brazil and Rio de Janeiro grows, as a port.
4. In 1763 the national capital was moved to Rio. There was an economic crisis when the flow of gold diminished and a drop as well in sugar cane production. But coffee came to Brazil and the Portuguese Royal Family in 1808. Rio grew and prospered.
5. In 1815 Brazil is declared a "kingdom"; Dom Pedro I and II would rule through most of the 19th century via a Constitutional Monarchy.
6. The 19th century was the time of real growth in Rio: the National Theater, the National Library, the Rio Botanical Garden, the Emperors' Palms.
7. There was an increase in coffee plantations in Rio de Janeiro State and the economy grew. The most iconic street in old downtown Rio the "Rua do Ouvidor" was established; the system of transportation developed (the trains by the British), and the Ferry to Niteroi.
8. In 1889 with Independence Rio was declared Capital of the New Republic.
9. In 1906 they developed its showcase avenue, "Avenida Rio Branco".
10. In the mid-20th century there were migrants to Rio from the dry Northeast, highways built, skyscrapers in Rio, residential districts, financial centers. Rio was second in economics only to São Paulo.

That was the "serious" stuff. I showed these images during the talk and had a lot of personal stories and anecdotes.

1. Downtown, Santos Dumont Airport
2. Glória, Passeio Público, Aterro Park on a Sunday
3. Airport, Glória, Flamengo, Botafogo, Yatch Club, Sugar Loaf, Copa, Fort, Ipanema-Leblon, Dois Irmãos, São Conrado
4. Cristo Redentor – Corcovado
5. Cristo and a little joke
6. Botafogo Bay and Sugar Loaf from Corcovado, favela on hill to left
7. Cable car to Sugar Loaf taken from Corcovado
8. Old Cable Car in 1967: rain, floods, generators out, car stalled in air Today: modern, generators
9. Copacabana in 1966
10. Sidewalks of Rio: Mosaic from Robert Burle Marx, Landscape artist for Brasilia. Walk on black or white and "do the samba."
11. Ipanema on a nice day: "frescobol," beach etiquette. Twenty minutes to settle into your group and Posto.
12. Ipanema at dusk. Girl from Ipanema now a grandmother.
13. New Year's Eve. Copacabana
14. Umbanda, New Year's Eve
15. Getting ready for Carnival, 1967
16. Salgueiro "Passista" my photo and cover of "Manchete"
17. Old Senate Rio
18. Confeitaria Colombo
19. Bonde, street car to Santa Teresa, "Orféu Negro"
20. Maracanã Football Stadium. 1950, lose to Uruguay. Win in 1958.

There were a lot of jokes and laughter and adventurers were ready to see those sights and hit those beaches. AT, IA, Steve, Amy and all of us had great things planned for them and hopefully a surprise or two.

The following "List of Dates of Monuments" was printed just for reference and did not enter the talk, but we would see many of them.

1565. City is founded: São Sebastião do Rio de Janeiro its official name.

1743. The "Paço Imperial" was built in the Old Praça 15 area facing the bay.

1750. The Carioca Aqueduct

1783. The "Passeio Público" near Glória.

1808. Rio was now capital of the Kingdom with the Braganças.

1811. Candelaria church was built.

1822. Rio became the capital of an Independent Brazil.

1854. Catete Palace was built in Flamengo (place of suicide of Getúlio Vargas in 1954); It would be the national palace until Brasília opened in 1960.

1858. Central do Brasil Train Station opened. It was the British who brought the white linen suit to Brazil; became national dress.

1877. The Trolley Car "O Bonde" to Santa Teresa in service

1884. The Corcovado railroad was started, but there was no Christ figure yet.

1904. Avenida Rio Branco was finished.

1909. The Teatro Municipal was finished.

1922 The Hotel Glória was completed.

1923. The Copacabana Palace was completed as well as Parque Guinle.

1926. The Hippodrome "Hipódromo" or race track in Laranjeiras was finished.

1931. The Cristo Redentor Statue was completed.

1936. Santos Dumont Airport was completed.

1940. The PUC was completed, Pontifical Catholic University. The 1940s: casino gambling was legal; some say 1947 the best year to live in Rio.

1950. Maracanã Soccer Stadium is opened but with a surprise loss to Uruguay. Brasil would only win the cup in 1958 with Pelé and Garrincha.

1960. The national capital is moved to Brasília. I lament: the national legislature building on Avenida Rio Branco, an architectural jewel, is torn down. Cinelândia in its place.

1961. Tijuca Forest is developed for tourism. Also "Edificio Avenida Central" then Rio's biggest skyscraper.
1965. Flamengo Aterro Park is built.
1972. The Petrobras Building is built; its home base.

2:00 p.m. Eli presented a wonderful talk with images on the screens and sound and video clips. Rio de Janeiro is known for Carnival, and Carnival is known for samba, and samba largely comes from the descendants of the slaves in Brazil, so Eli did a short history of slavery, (Harry would do the History of all this later at sea after Rio), its accompanying music and instruments, the origin and evolution of "samba," the highlights of Carnival. I had talked of my carnival experience earlier getting response and questions from some of the guests, i.e. did you meet Gina Lollobrigida or Brigitte Bardot? Mr. Diderot laughed and said he had!) He ended with what we call MPB or Brazilian Popular Music of the 1960s and now and showcased its most famous singers and composers, including Chico Buarque de Holanda.

That night we showed the BBC documentary, "God, Football and Carnival" in the lounge at 8:00 p.m. It really brought to life all I had talked about in the "Introduction to Rio," a great start. Adventurers were set be rest up and be up early tomorrow for a spectacular view of the harbor entering Rio, seeing the Sugar Loaf and Corcovado and then the fun begins.

At 9:00 I went to Amy's room where she had two telephones, one the ship's line, and I took a deep breath and called Chico Buarque. The maid answered, I identified myself as "Arretado," and she laughed and said she would put Chico on right away. Lucky he was home. He was duly surprised by my call and wondered where in the hell I was calling from. When I explained it was from the "International Adventurer" expedition ship and we would be docking in Rio tomorrow morning he couldn't believe it. I briefly explained my job, the fact the DOPS had allowed the visa for cultural reasons but no research! Ha. Could I talk to him at home tomorrow evening and I had this wild idea of a sort of adventure for him on the IA, if he could to cancel anything for July 21ˢᵗ evening and night and the next day to Parati. He said concerts and jobs were at a minimum now due to you know what, so no problem there, but what a surprise, yes, we'd have a great reunion with Marieta tomorrow night. Did I want him to call Cristina Maria? (I don't think Amy could hear the conversation but I just said maybe we could see later.) All set up to be at his house for dinner at 7 p.m.

We were both excited and I said I could let Amy know if he would be coming aboard when I got "home" to IA tomorrow night. I think she was as excited as I was.

24

RIO, A GREAT CITY, AND SURPRISES

Entering Rio

July 19th. Most everyone took the advice from the talk and was on deck as we rolled in from the north and made the big swing to the right into Guanabara Bay. You could see Sugar Loaf in the distance off to the left and the tiny cable cars up and down, the Christ Statue and Corcovado in the midst to the right, and the Rio downtown skyline closer to the left. Some say one of the major sights of the world. On the right there was beautiful beach and Niterói. Some passengers new to Brazil thought it might be Copacabana (it had skyscrapers in back). I said, good guess, but no cigar. Rio probably has a dozen such beaches. The naturalists were out in force, the sky full of gulls and Frigate Birds, and there were porpoise sightings (an amazing thing in polluted Guanabara Bay but they manage to survive). Captain Tony put me on the speaker phone to point out sights, a couple of which I didn't know, but for sure the ferry boats back and forth from Rio to Niteroi and the downtown, including the St. Benedict's Monastery downtown in the old port. And straight ahead in the mist, the huge Rio-Niteroi Bridge one of the "jewels" of the military government's projects for Brazil.

We all trooped back in for a hearty breakfast and then got packs, cameras, binocs and water bottles ready for the morning excursions. Split into 4 groups once again, two off to Corcovado, two to Sugar Loaf and then vice versa, everyone back to the ship for lunch. My van would start at Corcovado.

Magnificent Toucan at Cog Train Station

CORCOVADO. We wove through morning traffic to the cog train station at Corcovado in the Cosme Velho part of town, and it was crowded. Our group was asked to wait in the small "garden" to the side. That was not all bad because when we looked up in the trees there they were: two full-grown Magnificent Toucans in all their glory staring down at us. You can imagine: adventurers with all the cameras out; even I got a shot or two with my small Power Shot. Hungry in spite of that starter breakfast on board, I got a Brazilian treat variation: a long hot dog with onions, mustard and then topped with corn and green peas! No matter, I was starved. Steve got our tickets and handed them to each as we boarded the cog train.

Christ and Coca Cola

But everyone was taking in the sights: the tourist shops with Carioca string bikinis, posters with Jesus beside a big Coca-Cola sign and my favorite: Carioca humor in bumper stickers. One in particular, translated: "If you star does not shine, **** it, light a candle."

The train loaded and began its slow journey to the top, with Rio samba musicians entertaining all the tourists. The vegetation was dense to the side, but looked dry and a bit worn, the main fruit being the "jaca," maligned by many in Brazil as messy and not particularly good tasting. There were just a few flowers, red Hyacinths. The "Corcovado" or hunchback mountain is tall, about 2400 feet above sea level, made of solid granite, and very close to city center. The famous Christ statue itself was not put in place until 1931, a result of some Catholic charity work. Unforgettable for me was the time I saw on Brazilian TV the statue maintenance guys out of a tiny door on one of the arms, sitting with legs over the side and listening to transistor radios! Terrifying.

O Cristo Redentor, Corcovado

Up on top at the cog way upper station, and it took 20 minutes to get there, you can take an elevator to the floor of the base of the statue or go up a long series of very high concrete steps; I did the latter and it made for a good workout in the early Carioca heat and humidity. We kept an eye out for adventurers who were taking it slowly, some saying next time they would do the elevator. At the top it was an amazing awe-inspiring sight – the concrete avant-garde Christ Statue looming above us for 125 feet, and the 240 degree view below (I had taken slides before of it all, but you do the same thing every time you visit). I'll do the imaginary semi-circle for all: to the east of the Christ, the North Zone and the huge Maracanã Soccer Stadium, the downtown and its skyscrapers to the south and east, the Bay in the far distance to the east with the Rio - Niterói Bridge, then the long succession of beaches around Rio.

Pão de Açúcar, Botafogo

South Zone, Rio

In the South zone you begin with Glória, then the long Flamengo, then the gorgeous but polluted Botafogo, the granite hills and tunnels (Sugar Loaf on the left) then the "pearl" of Copacabana, the Military Fort at its end guarding the entrance to Rio, then now famous Ipanema and Leblon Beaches, the Dois Irmãos (Two Brothers) rocks, then the ocean beaches stretching west and south, São Conrado and then Barra, the "new" Copacabana for Rio's ultra-wealthy. How many rolls of film did you say?

It was crowded, a regular "Babylon" of languages and faces, not all polite; there was a bit of jostling to get to the wall at the edge for photos, but if you waited a bit you got your chance. IA staff made ourselves present to take photos of the adventurers and with them, and just keep an eye out. Wonky once again was right up to the edge and on the verge of leaning too far over, but Buck was right there to grab him if necessary, and me. No pickpockets were seen (they never are) or experienced, but we had warned everyone to take precautions. The view that morning was spectacular, the mist burning off to reveal the Rodrigo de Freitas Lagoa down to the right and Ipanema and Leblon in the distance but mainly Botafogo straight ahead and then Urca and Sugar Loaf. I've not traveled the world, but adventurers say this was certainly in the top ten sights!

I did get away for a moment and had a chance to join Harry Downing for a "cafezinho." He said he was a happy camper, doing his usual tasks aboard with library and zodiacs coming up in Parati, true, with fewer talks but with over two hundred AT trips under his belt he was not worried about that. He would be doing two or three talks on Atlantic history, but said once again this was his education for much of Brazil and was thoroughly enjoying my talks, "insider" information and enthusiasm. I returned the compliment saying what a pleasure just to hear him perorate on things from a Continental point of view. To that he said "Cheers!" and raised his coffee cup for a refill. After our trip he was set to continue on to South Africa, the Portuguese Route to India, eventually Macau and Japan. Then IA would head to the South Pacific, Australia and New Zealand. I said I hoped there would be time for at least one more talk to get to know each other before we ended in Porto Alegre. "Here, here! And I've been thinking of a plan for Adventure Travels that might involve you. We'll talk later on board." Hmm.

We herded cats and got everyone back aboard the cog train and waited for them, now more relaxed, to do a bit of shopping down below. One adventurer slipped and fell on the uneven sidewalk outside the Cog Station, skinned and bruised his knee badly but Steve was right there with a first aid kit, so all was well. The best thing – they all got pictures of the Toucans. The hot dog lady told me they are not always there and in fact may vanish for a year or two. Great luck we had!

We piled into the vans and drove straight south through busy Botafogo and São Clemente street where I was able to point out "old" embassy row (they were all in Brasília now, another story), but the mansions still providing the consulate people a place to rest their weary heads. The main sight I wanted folks to see was the Casa de Rui Barbosa which was my research center in Rio, a library and research center on the old grounds and mansion of Rui, a diplomat, candidate for President, one of the founders of the Hague in the Netherlands, precursor to the United Nations and a "polyglot!" Brazilians raved of his capacity in English ("He could give lessons to the Queen of England"). A total accident, the modest, looked-down-upon "Literatura Popular em Verso" ["Literatura de Cordel"] found a home there because someone wanted to preserve "popular speech of Northeastern Brazil," or at least that was the excuse.

SUGAR LOAF. We came out on the terrifically busy six lanes of traffic between downtown and Copacabana, cut into the left lanes and headed to the "peninsula" of Urca to the Sugar Loaf cable car terminal. Known as "Pão de Açúcar" in Portuguese (because of the similarity in shape to the old sugar cane molds for raw, hard sugar in the Northeast), the granite rock rises about 1300 feet above its entrance to the Bay of Guanabara in Rio. Truly an iconic site, its cable cars take people from the base of Babilônia Hill (scene of the "favela" of the same name in the movie "Black Orpheus") to Urca Hill, then a second, longer ride to the top of Sugar Loaf. If you get proper weather the views are the best in Rio, but clouds, smog, and fog can and do come. I was on the original cable car in 1967 when storms cut off electricity in Rio de Janeiro and we were stranded in the breeze for a few minutes (those old cars started in 1912) before the emergency generators cut in, but new, large, plexiglass windowed cars allow us 360-degree views in 1972.

There is no better cultural image to show the entrance to the cable cars to the iconic Sugar Loaf mountain than the gorgeous macaw of semi-precious stones in the entrance lobby. I have not mentioned that Brazil is perhaps a world leader in the mining, cutting and selling of topaz, amethyst, aquamarine and tourmaline stones. As a young student in Rio in 1967 a girl friend's mother who admired such things arranged for me to buy a handful of the cut stones for a pittance; everyone I knew, my mom, my sister and my girl friend all got stones for gifts. They had to arrange to mount them, costing as much as the stones!

I don't know which is better or more exciting, Corcovado or Sugar Loaf, maybe a draw, apples and oranges, but the cable cars were far more exciting then the cog train up and down through the forest. There were long lines, tourists from all over Brazil and the world! It is a bit scary, maybe, depends on the person, but just plexiglass between you and the ground a few hundred feet down, and the only noise the breeze or wind through the cable car windows. We were whisked up to Urca Hill, got off, walked a long path lined with tropical plants and trees to another building, all open air, to get on cable car number two.

Cable Car to the Top of Sugar Loaf

This time if you face forward and I suggested that to adventurers, you see the dense remains of the Atlantic Tropical Rain Forest below, the big granite rock ahead of you and the slow gradual climb toward it, passing the cable cars coming down. To the left is spectacular Botafogo Bay and then you arrive. It seems futuristic, a James Bond flick was filmed up here.

Copacabana from Sugar Loaf

We were allowed thirty minutes up on top and you needed it all to take in for the first time the full view of the crescent of Copacabana to the south and west, the entrance to the Bay of Guanabara and then the vast expanse of Guanabara Bay to the east and north, once again, downtown with Santos Dumont City Airport Shuttle flights between Rio and São Paulo, and the Bridge. Closest was the bay at Botafogo with the sailing boats, the tall buildings and then straight back, Corcovado in the distance.

Jack and Buck were both on top as I was, and we all walked to the other side of the cable car building to a small "forest" on top, looked for birds but just found what I think were sparrows. This was a first for both fellows; it would be more fun down on Urca Rock and its café on the return. Ronaldo the videographer had tracked me down back on Corcovado and here as well and did what turned out to be a spectacular clip with the bay and Corcovado in the background. I had great fun talking (flirting?) with a group of about twenty young ladies from Porto Alegre on their first trip to Rio to see the sights, er, Portuguese practice you might say.

Marmoset – Saguí – Sugar Loaf   Marmoset Cleaning Up
                                   Ice Cream Sundae

It's always sad to leave the top and get back in that cable car, but what a view and thrill down to Urca Hill. There was a scheduled break of almost 20 minutes, time to get a "cafezinho," ice cream or a cold beer. But it was here we saw an incredibly beautiful bird, all red, and the birders were snapping away. More exciting for Buck and really for everyone was the half dozen or so "Saguí" or Marmoset monkeys hanging around the restaurant and making nuisances of themselves. The minute customers left a table, they were on it, turning the ice cream sundae bowls upside down and licking them. Snap, snap, snap, click, click, click went the cameras! The Naturalists including Buck and Kelly would be out to the Golden Lion Tamarin Reserve in a day or two, so this was a good warm-up.

Everyone by now was a bit tired, hot for sure, and the vans awaited down below. I enjoyed the ride back to the ship on what amounted to my old bus route taken so many times to downtown and research at the National Folklore Center: through Botafogo along the Bay, around the curve in Flamengo (near the apartment building where I spent my first days in Rio in luxury in 1966 and later on stowed my Brazilian rosewood guitar bought with savings from living frugally for six months in the Northeast). Then through Gloria and the great view of the Igreja da Glória up the hill. Then up Avenida Rio Branco past Cinelandia and the Teatro Municipal and finally past the Benedictine Monastery near the port.

P.M. July 19th.

Everyone showered and had the regular buffet lunch before piling into vans once again but then a long p.m. walk to major sights in downtown Rio. Water jugs, cameras and a raincoat or umbrella were suggested as well as good walking shoes. The vans drove us to the Lapa area (we would return to the Scenarium Night Club tomorrow tonight) and let us all out in front of Rio's Metropolitan Cathedral.

RIO'S METROPOLITAN CATHEDRAL

Rio Metropolitan Cathedral   Interior of the Cathedral

After Sugar Loaf and Corcovado in the morning we visited Rio's Modern Cathedral in downtown Rio, a conical structure which reminded me of the U.S. space capsule of John Glen fame in the Air and Space Museum on the Mall in Washington, D.C. They claim the cathedral was inspired by Mayan Pyramids! It was built from 1964 to 1979 during the military regime and is quite a sight with its conical form and the many rows of stained glass on the inside (four rectilinear "the light of the Four Gospels?" - you hope for a sunny day) and ultra-modern statuary inside. It is dedicated to the patron saint of Rio, St. Sebastian, and carries his name. It is almost 100 meters across and a height of almost 75 meters, in other words, huge. There are wooden benches with no kneelers (seating capacity 20,000, standing 5,000), avant-garde statues of saints and Jesus on the Cross as well as an outstanding modern version of St. Francis. If it is not sunny the immediate impression is of an immense dark, gloomy place, but when that sun comes out it does an about face and is startling in its beauty.

An added scene I pointed out outside the Cathedral entrance is an iconic part of old Rio, the old public telephone booths. Brazilian humor rules: the Brazilians called the booths "the big ear" or "orelhão" and of course the first and most common greeting is "Oi!" ["Hi!".]

THE PETROBRAS BUILDING AND NATIONAL POLITICAL SCANDAL

Adjacent to the Cathedral is a landmark once symbolizing the grandeur and progress of modern Brazil – the glass and steel ultra-modern Petrobrás building – the home of one of Brazil's largest bureaucracies (in a country famous for its bureaucracy), the national oil company. Brazil's economic fortunes took an upturn in recent decades when large pools of oil were discovered in deep water off shore in the Atlantic ("The oil is ours"); since then a massive drilling effort has taken place with the huge floating oil rigs one sees from Bahia to Rio Grande do Sul. That's the good news. The bad news is that it has brought in huge amounts of income and the opportunity for Brazil's favorite pastime: political and economic corruption on a scale unimaginable even in Brazil. Private contractors for services and construction overcharged the company, "oiling" the squeaky hinges of Petrobras. My research on the modest "Literatura de Cordel" even got into the act, the poets writing and publishing dozens of fiercely satiric story-poems on the scandals including the "money in the shorts" incident when a money launderer was caught in one of the international airports with, well, his shorts stuffed with 100-dollar bills.

"CONFEITARIA COLOMBO," RIO'S TEA SHOP

Belgian Glass Mirrors in the Confeitaria   Art-Deco Stained-
Glass Ceiling

What we did not miss, and it truly was another highlight of that short afternoon in Rio was the planned visit to the "Confeitaria Colombo," a cultural and gastronomic highlight of the city. You could actually just walk two or three blocks from the Petrobrás Building. Founded in 1894 with Art Deco and "Belle Époque" architecture and décor it soon became THE gathering spot for socialites, politicians, intellectuals and artists and the aspiring public for afternoon tea, parties and social moments and great food especially the desserts. It was the primary spot in Rio to see and be seen. The huge mirrors from Belgium with the Brazilian rosewood frames, the gorgeous stained-glass ceiling plus the food, great demitasse coffee and desserts made it a thriving place, still the same today with IA's visit.

OLD DOWNTOWN RIO

On that rainy afternoon in 1972 after the "Confeitaria" we were not blessed by the Brazilian weather gods; there was light to heavy rain a good part of the afternoon. We donned our raincoats and pulled out the umbrellas and did a long walk through the old part of downtown Rio de Janeiro; one must know where one is going and have some knowledge of the 19th century to appreciate it. The walking excursion passed the old Portuguese Royal Palace. The palace was created in Rio in 1743 and came into prominence when Portugal was under the control of Napoleon Bonaparte and the Portuguese royal family fled to Brazil in 1808. Portugal only was freed when British General Wellington helped patriots in Portugal throw out Napoleon in 1814. Alas, there was no time to go inside.

A few other landmarks of that plaza remain but I think it is more important to talk about a couple of Brazilian cultural jewels that I pointed out to those stragglers on the tour (the group leader missed such sights or did not want to talk about them.) I was, as usual, bringing up the rear, watching for IA stragglers with a tendency to wander off the chosen path when curiosities arose. And they did.

This is where Carmen Miranda of musical and cinematic fame originally lived in Rio; Carmen was from Portugal, naturalized with her family in Rio and became that "kitsch" national icon with the fruit on her hat and "pseudo" Bahian dress.

A SURPRISE ENCOUNTER WITH THE NUMBERS' RACKET ["O JOGO DO BICHO"]

This small moment on the tour has an importance far beyond its brevity. Our guide was too busy to point out a fellow in blue jeans, long-sleeve shirt, leaning on a windowsill with a pencil in his hand and a notebook, but Mick Gaherty noticed and thought "Aha!" This is a national phenomenon: a "bicheiro" or numbers' racket salesmen of the illegal (but what else, nationally popular) lottery. These guys don't have offices but do their bookkeeping on the streets near their customers. It's a major part of Brazilian folklore, the lottery coming from a ticket procedure at the national zoo in the 19th century in Rio de Janeiro when folks buying tickets to get in received the ticket receipt with an animal image on it — lion, bear, giraffe, ostrich and the like - for a door prize. Like so many things Brazilian, that is, accidental, the ticket scheme was "borrowed" by hoodlums and evolved into today's multi-million dollar national "illegal" lottery. I can't begin to explain it all but can say it has become an important part of Brazilian folklore: people regularly interpret their dreams of animals into hunches for buying that day's lottery ticket. The lottery has a reputation for being the most honest corruption in all Brazil, it you win you get your money! Tickets are hand-written "chits" you take back to your dealer the next day and get your cash! The most common bet is one "real" or about 50 cents U.S.D. So, we at IA walked right by one of these "businessmen" at work. An aside: it is widely rumored and accurate that the huge national Carnival celebration with the Samba Schools and their parade has been sponsored with huge wads of cash by the "bicheiros" now a crime syndicate in Rio.

CANDELARIA CHURCH, ICON AND NATIONAL TRAGEDY

And finally, on our way back to the ship we walked by another iconic church in Rio, "A Candelaria" (with a female impersonator swishing by outside), the church built over the years after 1775, Baroque façade and Neo-Classic interior, known for being inaugurated by King João VI of Portugal while in Brazil fleeing Napoleon. It was also known in modern times in recent years for the "Candelaria Massacre," a planned operation by para-military or off-duty police to "disappear" the many street children who slept at night in the doorways and along the walls of the church. Many of the latter were murdered in cold blood and it became a national scandal. The "cordel" story-poems told it all for their public in Rio!

THE BENEDICTINE MONASTERY ["O MOSTEIRO BENEDITINO"]

Interior, Benedictine Monastery, Rio

The city tour that afternoon ended with a truly important, historic and iconic part of the city of Rio de Janeiro – the Benedictine Monastery – begun in 1590 donated from land on Benedictine Hill in downtown Rio to two Benedictine monks from the famous monastery in Bahia. Construction throughout the 17th and 18th centuries resulted in the Baroque masterpiece. Equally famous was the Benedictine school to its side with some of the most famous Brazilians as graduates including Pixinguinha, Noel Rosa and Heitor Villa – Lobos of Brazilian music fame. I had a private tour of the monastery in 1967 through connections at my rooming apartment that culminated in lunch in the refectory with the monks and eating in silence with scripture readings. IA adventurers were fortunate to have this visit including the beautiful "mangueira" trees outside with the splendid orchids in their branches. Kelly was along and raved, "I've rarely seen such beauties in full bloom and in such a natural setting!"

Most of us were pretty miserable with a 15-minute walk from the Monastery back to "Adventurer," wet with sweat and rain. There was plenty of time to shower, take a nap, have a nice dinner on board and then go out once again later in the evening to one of Rio's most famous "churrasco" restaurants. It is one of Brazil's great culinary experiences – dozens of salads, cuts of beef, pork, chicken, black beans, farofa, and icy beer. Eli had arranged all this and led the group. Sorry I missed it. Tonight is my "leave time" with Chico Buarque de Holanda and his wife Marieta.

25

REUNION WITH CHICO AND MARIETA

I took a taxi to their place in Laranjeiras, arriving after weaving through some city traffic about 7:30. After ringing the buzzer, the gate slid open and I heard the familiar voice almost yelling "Oi Arretado! Que sorpresa! Que prazer." Chico was bounding down the steps from the house to the sidewalk, a big smile on his face and a big "abraço." (All was in Portuguese.) I answered the pleasure was mine and was just grateful he was free to see me and happy to see me. Marieta joined us, a Carioca embrace with all those "air kisses," and she motioned us into the spacious and comfortable living room. Chico, not changed a bit, immediately called the maid and ordered cachaça and Brahma Choppe which did not take long in coming along with all kinds of "aperitivos."

Pleasantries were exchanged, the kids were fine, both now in pre - school, Marieta was full-time in taking care of them, their close knit circle of friends maintained, but really a lull in professional activity since I had been there last year and all that business I wrote about in "Letters III." Chico and friends were playing in some local clubs, doing interviews on music on the radio, but nothing new or controversial since "Cálice" and obviously I knew about that (Chico had read "Letters III"). No big news on protests or leftist violence because there was none. Life as usual – futbol, the beach and carnival. The "pharaonic projects" were moving along. (I told Chico of meeting the road engineer in Manaus and how I was apprised of the construction "difficulties.") He laughed and said, "Just wait. Much more to come. But we are really shocked to see you, what a surprise!"

I told them about routine at U. of N. after I got home last fall, normal, a "hiatus" with Molly, and then this chance for a summer gig. It came out of the blue, but a great opportunity to do something different, but mainly to get back to Brazil with AT cutting the red tape to get me a "Business Visa and Sea Man's Card." I talked a long while about AT, the IA and the "gig," describing the ship, the people and the places seen so far, emphasizing what a great experience it had been with all the naturalists and an education for me. Both he and Marieta were a bit envious of the whole thing, the places and experiences in Brazil, but the glamour of the ship and the education! That's where I jumped in and made the proposal.

"Chico, I have already set some wheels turning and have initial support for a project. Here it is: you, your singer Gini, and maybe two backup musicians, and Marieta too can be involved. You would come on board June 21st the day after tomorrow; we would have cocktails and a nice dinner; our chef is from Italy and maybe I can swing an Italian dinner! I promise you would not be hounded for autographs, then we would do a reprise of "Mistakes of Our Youth," you, Gini and I and the guys and some of that Rock n' Roll and then maybe one hour of the 'old favorites,' simple sambas. I would do a lot of translating so you wouldn't have to be worried about English, although I know you can hold you own. We could give you a tour of the ship and have time for some socializing in the lounge later, maybe two hours until midnight. You would have two cabins, one for Marieta and Ginni, and one for you and the guys, or however you might want. AT can come up with $800 and our world music guy $200 more if you give him permission to film the session for his weekly TV program to be aired next Fall. I'm thinking, it's not at all what you would earn in a regular concert but you would have great fun that evening, sleep on the ship as we move on down to Parati the next morning. You would get off in Parati and have to arrange your own transportation back to Rio. What have I left out? Oh, yeah, I forgot our travelers will be wanting to have souvenirs, buying some of your cassettes or CDs, especially "Mistakes." Você topa?"

Chico howled with laughter, looked over at Marieta and said, "Do you want a couple of nights away from the kids?" She said, "You must be kidding. Certo! But what about permission from the DOPS and ITAMARATI?" I said, "We have someone who can arrange all that tomorrow if you give me the names and contact numbers; IA guarantees you go aboard one night, get off in Parati and won't try to skip the country!"

Chico said, "Isto é mesmo um barato! [This is really a hoot!] The answer is hell yes! Miguel, I've got to get on it right away; some of my band might not be free, but I think they will jump at the chance. One thing though, it's got to be low key, maybe we can term it a 'diplomatic cultural exchange' for the benefit of Brazil and MPB. I'm thinking AT and your World Music guy could take that tack. And that would be the explanation to the DOPS and the government. The Left here would be more amenable to that, downplaying just associating with the USA, capitalist interests and the Military's interests. It's tricky and Miguel we are all walking a tightrope here, I think you can appreciate that. But also, honestly, $1000 dollars is not "hay" right now for us and my guys, not our old "usual," but combined with a ride on the IA, porra! We can just call it 'another way to have a weekend in Parati,' all the Brazilians will get that."

I made a quick call back to the ship to Amy, excitedly repeated what Chico and I had discussed, asked her to tell Captain Tony, Steve, contact Eli and even Chef Reynaldo if IA was amenable. I said we had talked about $500, Eli $200; I would add the $300 if need be. Chico interrupted and gave me the phone number of General Goeldi in Censorship and the head DOPS agent. He would call both early tomorrow, let us know at the ship by noon (we would be out to the beach) if it's green light or not. Amy was really excited, "AT and IA have never had an artist of this magnitude on board, it is well worth the investment and Eli will be overjoyed. Why don't you stop by the room tonight and we can settle on plans? I would need to get the ball rolling tomorrow morning before the beach excursion." (I had thoughts of trying to contact Cristina Maria yet tonight and that squelched that, but it turned out okay after some news from Chico.)

We talked some more, Chico thinking we needed a rehearsal before the ship, me saying even if we were a bit rusty, it would just be a sing 'along for Rock n' Roll and his "samba" would be like falling off a log, and minimum equipment. Our sound guy Willie would help them set up in the lounge for the post-dinner performance, but everyone understanding it was casual and spur of the moment. We left it at that. He brought up Cristina Maria just, he said, because of old times. She and Marieta were longtime friends and Marieta had the latest. Cristina was now at the end of second year law school at the UFERJ, the Federal University of Rio de Janeiro, had no particular boy friend but was intent on finishing school first. That would be another full year plus Bar Exams. She did have admirers, and one in particular, a fellow law student with a family pedigree way back to the Getúlio Vargas and Juscelino Kubitschek era, headed for a glamorous business or political career whichever and wherever he chose. I thought to myself of our meetings of last year and how we left it; there would be no changing our DNA, Cristina the patriot, Mike the patriot. I thought to myself, "Mike, let it be. Put it to rest. Other fish to fry." And there were many.

Déjà vu all over again! Outside Chico's gate instead of the taxi I called was, uhh, the black DOPS car! Only one possibility I think – Heitor Dias, super sleuth and now friend. Sure enough, Heitor opens the door, gets out, smiles and gives me that Carioca bear hug, saying he's glad I'm back, he's missed me, and we've got a lot to talk about, offering to give me a ride back to the ship, but with a stop for a drink or two at the "pé-sujo" in Copacabana. Not an invitation to refuse, I hopped in and said, "Just beer for me Heitor, it's already been a long evening."

The driver let us off a block from the bar and when we walked in several guys waved to him saying good to have him back. One waved, came over, and seeing me, said "Pois é! O Arretado de novo! Cuidado com a companhia deste rapaz!" ["Be careful with this guy's company!"] They must have been good friends because both laughed. After we sat down and were drinking the "choppe," we had a welcome-back talk of sorts. I was ill at ease just because of the time factor, but Heitor loaned me his police phone to call Amy. He said it's business as usual, he's had communication with Odálio in Manaus and Sérgio in Recife. "I'm glad you are here, I didn't know when I would see you again after last time, but you've got your ducks in a row and all the right papers, so welcome my friend. Life can't be all bad on that "luxo" of a ship! But porra you're back at Chico's! That's a red flag."

"Heitor, Chico told me everything has been calm since 'Cálice' days, no upsets and no visits needed downtown. He's been low key and has seen the light of the times I think. Me too, I wouldn't even have been here except for that big break from AT to do lectures on Brazil. But since you found me, so to speak, I'll give you the early word on what we are cooking up, and it's not even a bit dubious." I gave him the plan for the music on board, getting the permissions tomorrow.

"Miguel, I'm just disappointed we won't have much time together. I know you had no reason to call me so I'm not offended, but since we are eyeball to eyeball, I'll just say it's pretty much like you say. Things, politically speaking, are pretty well battened down now, no elections in sight or promised, "censura" still the name of the game, but no riots, demonstrations or bombs, so we must be doing a pretty good job. Socially, I do visit Maria Aparecida's place now and again but I think I won't mention you. She might be offended you did not stop. We could go over there yet tonight, but it looks like it's a 'no go' for you."

"Heitor, a small point. This whole thing on IA is a job, and I'm a rookie, and I was fortunate I was able to get time off tonight to see Chico, but that was only to see about music and a possible show, and by the way, repeating, if it comes off we'll only be doing that Rock n' Roll and his old "A Banda" LP stuff. Chico is in no mood to make waves, except a few on down to Parati. I guess we'll only know maybe by noon tomorrow if we can pull it off."

"Miguel, if called upon I'll put in a good word for you. And I don't mind telling you I'm jealous of those colleagues of mine who have been on the ship." There was a pause.

"Heitor, things are coming fast and furious, but since Sérgio was on and no repercussions I'm thinking a drink and a quick tour tomorrow 5:30 p.m. sharp, of course, after I've cleared it with my boss with whom I am incidentally late to see now."

"Tit for tat my friend; I think I can help grease the wheels for tomorrow, but can you call me at noon sharp when there is more news and maybe I'll see you at 5:30. What clothes by the way? I can't go as a cop." "Slacks, maybe a nice polo shirt. Let's go, got to get back!"

I arrived about thirty minutes later than planned to see Amy, but it was all right. Adventurers had just returned from the "Churrascaria" and music, so the ship was busy. Amy was final checking outings for tomorrow, vans, security guards for the beach and a strict protocol for sticking together at the beach – one, big, white, foreign group and hopefully no robberies or assaults. She was excited to hear word for word the time with Chico. She greeted me with a long kiss and hug, offered a scotch and we sat on the divan and caught up. We left it with her making some early calls to General Goeldi and the **DOPS** before the beach. She said IA could do an Italian dinner the day after tomorrow regardless. And she added to not worry about the $300. For this, AT and IA could do the $800. "Get some sleep Arretado, you've earned it. Oh, no female contacts tonight?" "No boss, but I'll take you up on your offer." That was sealed with a nod and another kiss or two. "Off to bed, I'm joining you on the beach tomorrow so be ready for some fun; of course, the adventurers will be right beside us, so no funny stuff!"

26

SECOND DAY IN RIO, A "BIG PROGRAMA" AS THE BRAZILIANS SAY

July 20th. Sunday. IPANEMA BEACH AND THE HIPPY FAIR

Posto de Sol, Ipanema – Leblon

I was up early around 6 a.m., down for the early coffee and breakfast. The announcement came from Steve who put Amy on the intercom with specific instructions for the beach outing. She told everyone some basics: beach towel, sandals or thongs for the hot sand, sun tan oil, just enough cash for a soft drink or snack or two, and that IA security would be with us. Departure set for 8:30, early for Cariocas to get to the beach. She added that IA had lucked out, not only was there sunshine, but it was Sunday so the Hippy Fair should be in full swing in Ipanema off the beach. Lots of amazing stuff to buy and quality souvenirs, so take extra cash or a credit card for that; the vendors are used to the international crowd and accept plastic. **BUT WATCH YOUR STUFF!**

She stopped at the dining room, saw me, came over with a big smile and said it had been too long since she had a nice beach outing, but hoped we could do some body surfing together. She would meet me at the van at 8:30 and hoped to have some news from the General and **DOPS** by then. "Cross your fingers!" I was ready with my "gringo" boxer-style swim suit and stuff. There was a crowd at the departure door, even the naturalists looking for some "rays," but excited about the next day when nature, animals and birds would be the main feature.

Amy was in the bus, sat beside me, and said she had made the calls to the General's office and **DOPS** and left the inquiry about Chico Buarque. They took the details, said Chico had already called and they would have a response at 12:00 noon, so "hurry up and wait." Today adventurers traveled in a bus through fairly easy traffic the "back way" past the Lagoa and coming into the beach at Leblon, then turning left and following the roadway to Ipanema. What a sight! Harpoador Rock to the left, the long only slightly curving beach to the end of Leblon and the Dois Irmãos Rocks, and medium sized waves on a sparkling sunlit day. Every one piled out and instructions were given to meet at the bus at 11:30 sharp in Plaza General Osório at the Hippy Fair; no parking, just a pick up, so be on time!

We decided beach time would be until 10:30 and then on over to the Hippy Fair and back to the ship at 12:00. What a day and what a view when Amy took off her Carioca wrap and revealed what the naturalists had been talking about for weeks – a curvaceous body in a carioca green bikini (to match her eyes). It took a while for me to settle down; we made our "sand hill" beach accommodation carioca style (you kick the sand into a mound with your feet) put the beach mats on top and stretched out in the sun marveling at the surroundings – beach, Ipanema (and my old haunt the "Castelinho" just across the street and the famous "Garota de Ipanema" bar just down the way) and, well, the Cariocas at the beach. Even in July ("winter" in Brazil) with sunshine it was soon very warm and the sun which felt so good for a few minutes was bearing down. As promised, we went into the water, cold compared to Salvador, but refreshing, worked our way through the waves and did that body surfing (the Brazilians have a great saying, "fazer jacaré" ["making like an alligator]). It required some timing with the medium sized waves, but was all the exercise and swimming I needed for sure.

Like Amy said, "no funny business" turned out to be the "word," because adventurers were all around us. Several had talked to me and hinted about me and Amy, and not to be denied! The guy naturalists smiled and said, "Gaherty you seem to have won the lottery, for now anyway." We let the sun dry us off, did one more dip and it was time to get on over to the fair. It was just two blocks from where are group was, so we "herded" people along the great broad mosaic sidewalk seeing the sights. Oh, "Grouchy Lady," evidently recovered from the fall in Salvador, in her beach best for her age group was complaining we did not go to Copacabana, and there were a few others. I assured them all that the "in" beach in Rio now was Ipanema and once they saw the artisan work at the fair all would be forgiven, and that was the case. They had all heard "The Girl from Ipanema" and a couple made it to the bar.

I was a regular at the fair first time around in 1967 and again in 1969. This was not tourist "junk," but fine artisan work – paintings, colored glass sculptures of Toucans, Rio Churches, Sugar Loaf and Corcovado, all kinds of really good clothing – but my favorite was one Carioca artist who did leather work – engraving on leather - of intricate large maps of Old World and New World, of the Portuguese Caravels, and even the famous four master tall ship – the Cutty Sark. I used all my cash to get a beautiful Portuguese Caravel and would haul it home the end of the trip. The bus was jammed with happy adventurers, and most with arms full of good purchases. They later at CC would rave about the quality and the entire morning – this was the Brazil they had dreamed of.

One other minor event – Wonky wandered off with his big camera ostensibly to take shots of the whole scene and was shooed off by Ipanema guards when he was trying to get too close to the Carioca beauties on the beach. Disgruntled but smiling he whispered to me, "Mike, wait until you see my videos!" He would give me a private showing of the video later on the ship, and … not bad, not bad!

All was well, now with regular Sunday traffic, a noisy happy bus made its way back to the ship. Everyone in the showers at the same time, déjà vu again, cool showers! I was just dressing when the phone rang and it was a very happy Amy – great news! – the army and the censors and the DOPS all decided Chico was good for Brazil and the U.S.; it's on for tomorrow night! I called Chico right away, gave him the good news and set the time for his crew and equipment to be at the ship at 4:30 p.m. tomorrow; IA personnel would help with arrangements. There was one catch – he would have to make arrangements to pack up equipment and have someone get it all home before midnight, departure time for "Adventurer," and then he and friends back on board for the "ride" to Parati the next morning.

What to do about Heitor? I talked to Amy, Steve and Captain Tony, cleared the visit and called him, saying he would have to be at the ship at 5:30 sharp this afternoon for his "tour" and a quick drink and short tour of the ship, hoping he would go along with all that. We were on schedule to go to the Scenarium Night Club at 8:00. He agreed saying this was a big moment in his life and he would not miss it! Meanwhile I could not miss the p.m. Província "Favela" trip and Liberdade Samba event.

PROVÍNCIA "FAVELA" AND LIBERDADE SAMBA EVENT

July 20th. P.M. The vans headed out from the port, a short ride to Província "favela" or "community" as they now called them. Adventurers were warned: we would drive as far up as possible (Rio "favelas" are the poorest part of town but have the best views) but then there were no less than 80 tall concrete steps to the top. "Favela" security would be all along the way. We took it easy up the steps, resting, and all finally gathered at the top. This was a first for almost everyone, including myself (no forays in Rio "favelas" before), a real education.

Samba Performance, Província Favela

A Teenager Shows Us Samba Steps

Eli had arranged a show with the Favela Social Club kids and it was a doozy! These kids were prepping for the real thing – Carnival! Several varieties of samba, drumming, and a big cake and "caipirinhas" for adventurers. This was a highlight for many adventurers, being in a real Rio de Janeiro "favela" and they said the same to Steve, Amy and me later, and of course Eli who regularly "scouts" such things for his show. Even Wonky got his fill of pictures! All the residents were extremely friendly and I might add, appreciative; Leonel the diplomat sidled over to me and said that even for him it was an adventure. Diplomats do not usually visit "favelas." Eli left a large "donation" in the name of "Adventurer."

Pirated Electric Lines

Perhaps it was the view. One could see 160 degrees of that famous, poor part of Rio, looking east to the docks in the distance, then Guanabara Bay and the Rio – Niterói Bridge. The sky was filled with Frigate Birds. After the forty-five-minute performance, everyone was carefully escorted down to the vans. I was on follow up, but then encouraged by a police officer it would be quicker and easier "down the back way." Indeed, one saw the tiny rooms, some with color TV, pets, mainly lots of cats, the wash out on lines, and the tangled web of power lines, all "pirated" from the Rio's main electric lines.

It was just a few blocks to what looked like a big warehouse, but was indeed the "Home" of "Liberdade" one of the top samba schools in Rio. This is where it starts and ends – from the planning stage of the year's major theme for Carnival a few months away, the school song, the dozens of supporting role "wings" of the samba school, to the construction of the huge samba school parade floats. There was a very strong chemical odor, I think from the Styrofoam and the glue putting all the huge figures in place. We were in luck, all unplanned. Three or four floats were already complete, one a huge long serpent with a tiger's head!

Liberdade Samba School Front Line

Even though it was just July, most of the school dancers and participants were gathered in an adjoining huge pavilion, all in the gold Lamé costumes, for a recording of this year's theme song. Either these were the most "endowed" beautiful women in all Rio, or silicon treatments had been on sale! They were the "passistas" or front – line star dancers, and ten "hunks" just as impressive would dance with them. The recorded performance of their song along with twenty others from the other Samba Schools would be put on cassette tapes for sale all over Rio to put the Cariocas in the mood for the coming party over six months away. Once again, for many adventurers "this" made the trip; they had all seen nature all over the world, but never before a rehearsal for the world's biggest party – Carnival in Rio. It made me rethink my talk on Rio; I really did not get into Carnival that much. If there's a next time that will be changed! Many said they were coming back to Rio for the real thing!

Back to the ship at 4:15, everyone was instructed to get into their party clothes for tonight's samba performance at the big club in the Lapa District of Rio – once again all set up by Eli. We were indeed on his "turf" and he did not disappoint. For me there was barely time to clean up when the phone rang and Executive Officer Martim said there was a gentleman waiting at the foot of the entrance stairway saying he had an "appointment" with me. Porra! It had to be Heitor Dias.

I hustled down to the gangway, and sure enough, Heitor in Rio "casual;" I hardly recognized him. We got a temporary "visitor's" pass from Exec Officer Martim, he welcoming our visitor, and a quick but impressive tour of the ship. By then it was CC time, so I invited Heitor to join me for a couple of quick drinks in the lounge, introducing him as "a research colleague" in Rio. When Amy heard us talking in Portuguese, she joined us, and Heitor's eyes popped! "Agora, compreendo, o' Arretado, a vida deve ser boa, não é?" ["Now I get it! Oh, Arretado, life must be good, huh?"] I even introduced him to Leonel and friends, first reminding him who they were, and to "be cool." Fortunately, and understandably they had never met, so the "research colleague" cover was welcomed. Heitor even bullshitted them talking of our times in the research center at the Casa de Rui (ha!) He was agog with happiness saying once again what a thrill this was. "Nunca sonhei subir a bordo a tal maravilha. Obrigado Miguel, não esquecerei." ["I never dreamed of being on board such a marvel! Thanks Miguel, I will never forget it."] We talked of the rest of the time in Rio, the outings tomorrow and Chico and friends on board for an informal show tomorrow night, but "no politics, just Rock n' Roll and old samba." I managed to get him into the dining room for dinner and some icy "choppe," he marveling once again on that "boa vida" saying he would always remember it. He assured me he would give a glowing report to General Goeldi and that this went a long way to "cementing the good relations of Brazil and the United States." As I escorted him to the exit door, he and I both got a little emotional, hoping for a quick return for me to Brazil in better times. Once again he said, "Nunca tive um 'serviço' tão agrádavel pelo DOPS. Um abraço, amigo, e até a próxima." ["I never had such a pleasant assignment from the DOPS. An embrace, my friend, until next time."]

There was just time enough to change clothes, nice slacks and a polo and dress shoes for IA's and Eli's next extravaganza. Tonight would be …

THE SCENARIUM

Samba Band and Singers

It was "real" samba music from one of the best-known female Carioca samba singers and copious amounts of "caipirinhas" and lots of dancing. Eli and IA had arranged our own private room for her show. It was a bit sterile. Why? No Cariocas! Later that was resolved. The Club doubles as one of the best places for antiques in Rio and adventurers' eyes were wide open to walk from our salon to see all that. It was jammed with Cariocas, laughing, talking too loud, drinking and mainly dancing. From the second level where we entered one could look down and see the band and singers and a full dance floor. Big day again tomorrow, so I caught the 11:00 p.m. bus but understand a few adventurers and the naturalists made a night of it until 2:00 a.m. How do I know? All the bleary eyes at breakfast the next day.

27

LAST DAY IN RIO, BUT
WHAT A DAY!

July 21ˢᵗ. We had a big day planned; here it is. In the a.m. there would a group going with Buck Weylander to the Golden Lion Tamarin Reserve about two hours outside of Rio promising views of Brazil's most spectacular and near to extinction monkey. A second would go to the Rio Botanical Gardens and then hike up the trail in the Tijuca National Forest all the way to the viewpoint of Vista Chinesa. Kelly had to be there for the Gardens and flowers on the trail; Jack as well for the birds. A third option would be by AL Steve and Willie on a boat excursion in Guanabara Bay to investigate sea life - real dolphins managing to survive in those murky polluted waters and who knows what else. Another option would be the terrific ride on the Rio to Niterói Ferry and return with the view of Rio, Corcovado and Sugar Loaf, a nostalgia trip for many who had done the ferries at Istanbul and Hong Kong (adventurers get around!). CC with all its great things would be postponed until tomorrow night after Parati.

The highlight of late afternoon would be a surprise after cocktails in the lounge and a special all-Italian extravaganza from Chef Reynaldo and the dining staff: the presence of renowned Brazilian singer Chico Buarque de Holanda, a small band, and a mystery artist! And Brazilian "Brahma Choppe" beer and real "caipirinhas" courtesy of IA, a very special occasion.

THE RIO DE JANEIRO BOTANICAL GARDENS AND THE HIKE THROUGH THE TIJUCA FOREST TO THE "VISTA CHINESA" OVERLOOK

I was really excited about this, having just done it with Chico himself as guide a year ago. It would have been great to have him along, but it was not his style – he preferred the twice a week walk alone, moving fast up and down. The vans encountered major Rio traffic for the first time, bumper to bumper the back way to the Gardens. There were tourists to be sure, Brazilians and from around the world. Our guide was great and got along well with Kelly and Jack. We saw the Emperor Palms over 100 years old, tall and stately, planted during the time of Dom Pedro in the middle of the 19th century, all kinds of tropical plants (Kelly knew most), a small "pond" with Victoria Regina water lillies (we saw those it seemed a year ago in Manaus). The "pièce de resistance" were the bromeliads and orchids. I had been to the Gardens twice before and was given the Brazilian response: "They are not in bloom. Come back again." I came back and came back again, no luck. But not this time! All sizes and colors and Kelly admitting one of the best "garden" displays she had ever seen (adding that wild orchids in Colombia were even better); she knew the names of them all; adventurers were impressed and happy to see Kelly have her "day in the sun."

Then it all changed, even better. Another guide (and IA security along) took us to the back of the Gardens to the trail in the Tijuca National Forest. We had been advised it was steep and long; carry lots of water, and don't forget the cameras! The path, sometimes sandy gravel, sometimes road, wound its way past heavy forest and occasional waterfalls to the top. The guide explained this amazing forest had been planted in the 19th century to overcome the erosion of sugar cane and coffee growing up on top and a threat to Rio's water supply. The replanting was done in a smart way, using and transplanting original trees and plants from what remained of Brazil's Atlantic Rain Forest.

Jack and Kelly were, how shall I say, almost ecstatic. (The Brazilians had done something right for a change, listening to 19th century naturalists!) We frequently ran into animals across the trail or heard them; a couple were exotic – an agouti (like a big rat!), several Marmoset monkeys and a sloth and an armadillo! The guide said we didn't have to worry about "onças" [big cats], a joke, ha! The highlight was the birds, constant noise in the trees. Jack spotted a gorgeous blue throated hummingbird, but the prize was a small Toucan with amazing color, different from the bigger ones we saw at Corcovado. It had a yellow breast and blue – red bill and Jack knew its name an "araracarí – poca" or Saffron Toucan. He and Kelly said there were flycatchers, parakeets, tanagers and even warblers. What a haul! Oh, and Wonky was almost bitten by a snake when he stuck his head and camera a little too far into the underbrush, pulled out in time by Buck.

For the tired, thirsty adventurers who made it to the top we were treated to yet another of the views of Rio, some say the best. It was like that from Corcovado, but now with it in the distance in the mist - Corcovado, Botafogo Bay and a misty Sugar Loaf, the Rodrigo de Freitas Lake way down to the right and the whole long line of Ipanema – Leblon and the Dois Irmãos Rocks to the right. Everyone was bubbling with happiness on the way down and the bus ride back to the ship. A big "sucesso" as the Brazilians say. Amy was on board, very busy with arrangements for the evening and still setting up affairs for Parati tomorrow. Adventurers took the afternoon off, some still a bit in recovery from the samba club, but getting cleaned up and dressed up for the shindig that night. We would get Buck, Steve and Willie's news, including Buck's incredible photos of the Golden Lion Tamarins on CC tomorrow night.

CHICO MARIETA AND FRIENDS

I think there was a very unusual welcoming party for Chico and Marieta – the word had gotten out - Captain Tony, Exec Martim, Eli, Amy and I. The van with the equipment arrived and a car with Chico, Marieta,

Gini his great background singer, and two other musicians right on time at 4:30. Chico's first remark: "Porra, Arretado, que luxo! 'Bora! Vai ser uma noite inesquecível." ["Damn, Arretado! What luxury! Let's get going! It's going to be an unforgettable night."] They minimized equipment - very small amps and speakers, guitars, flute and drums. We got them on board, took them to their cabins, then to the lounge where Willie helped them set up (we wanted to be outside on the deck, but while "Adventurer" was docked and maybe with some discretion all would be inside.) In thirty minutes, it was all set.

There was no shortage of volunteers to give the short tour of "Adventurer," including a welcome by Captain Tony in Italian which both Chico and Marieta answered in kind. Amy and I led the tour, albeit short. Time was passing and it was getting close to 5:30. There would a formal introduction during cocktails and then allowing them to be with us, mainly me and Amy as "anfitriones" or hosts. The bar was open, top shelf scotch if you wanted it, and Chico helped make the "caipirinhas." The barman had been sure to set in several bottles of "Pitu," the most famous name in cachaça. Everyone wanted to meet this "famous Brazilian guy and his beautiful wife," but we did not want them to be overwhelmed, so it was definitely low key. Conversation was mainly about the ship, the adventurers and the "Around Brazil" trip. We filled them in on all our stops, surprises and that brought a great deal of laughter. Chico wanted in particular to know my role and all about my talks.

At 7:00 we all moved into the dining room for dinner, a special round booth reserved for Chico and friends, Amy and I. Captain Tony made sure Chef Reynaldo had good Italian wine flowing, courtesy of "Adventurer," and then a four-course Italian meal, the real thing. Anti-Pasto, pasta, veal parmigiana, formaggio, all "irrigated" with good Chianti, Tiramisu and wonderful café afterward and the orange flavored liqueur famous in Italy. Conversation was in Portuguese, much reminiscing of last year's "Mistakes of Our Youth" LP and concerts at the War Memorial, Rio-Niteroi Bridge, Iguaçu and Itaipu before the stuff hit the fan (the torture and death of the São Paulo journalist I wrote about in "Letters III"). Chico said he would tell me more after the music. The announcement came and we all were ready to go at 8:30 back in the lounge. The bar was open, and most everyone took advantage of it.

What a great time! I was the "emcee" introducing Chico, Gini the great backup singer, his guitarist-flautist, drummer, and Marieta sitting with Amy in the front row. I explained briefly the Chico – Mike "connection" with his song and "cordel" and how that evolved to the LP and concerts, and how incredibly fortunate we were this evening – a dream come true for all present (the lounge was packed - adventurers, Captain Tony and Exec Martim, the naturalists). Perhaps the best composer and performer of popular music and sophisticated samba in all Brazil! And the "mysterious guest singer - me!" That evoked some hoots and laughter. We launched into the old Rock n' Roll and suddenly the aisles were full of dancers and hilarity. Then Chico did a set of his "old favorites sambas" of "A Banda" era. And encores! No dancing this time, but rapt attention from all. Tears came to my eyes as we listened. Even without knowing Brazilian music and samba adventurers hailed him time and time again.

Eli was not left out and he took the podium to explain that the entire evening's performance was recorded by him and would be featured on his weekly World Music show back home in the Fall. Copies of the performance video would be available from him. And there was time for all to take home a souvenir – an LP or Cassette or CD of Chico's music. Sold out!

I forgot to say that after the performance Steve stepped up, thanked all and did a prep for Parati; adventurers were soon to have another great experience in one of Brazil's most favored vacation spots. Tomorrow morning in the bay, zodiacs into the port, and a fun day.

We lamentably closed up at 10:30 and Chico and the group packed up equipment, got it to the departure area and his people in a van loaded it up. Then it was back to the lounge for talk, more drinks, and a wonderful, I might say intimate conversation with all of us. As promised, there was no politics, at least not directly, just an agreement to enjoy the evening. There was no way we could not get caught up in that Brazilian moment. I told Chico of the group hike up into the Tijuca Forest to the "Vista Chinesa" and he promised he and I would do it again soon. We all wondered when that would be, not yet. Amy and Marieta really hit it off and Marieta wondered (in Portuguese) about Amy and me. What to say? Amy blushed and said "É o começo. Veremos." It was one of those moments you don't want to let go of, and conversation continued until way after midnight. All would get together for breakfast tomorrow a.m. before the Parati landing. Chico expressed cautious optimism that one day soon the "old" Brazil would be back to normal; that was the closest he even referred to the current situation.

Amy speaking for AT and Captain Tony for IA later expressed the joy of this "one-time" unforgettable event, all wishing we could do it again.

A last memorable event was when we all went out on deck to see the night -time departure of "Adventurer" from Rio. Lights on the downtown, Corcovado and Sugar Loaf in the distance, and lights on the tall buildings of Niterói on the way out. There was spontaneous applause by the adventurers alongside us. Amidst lots of "abraços" we all said goodnight and repaired to respective rooms, a little the worse for wear and all needing some sleep, with promises to talk again at breakfast.

28

ARRIVAL IN PARATI, THE FINAL BREAKFAST AND THE DAY

The Beautiful Entrance into Parati

July 22nd. Everyone was up early at 6:30 and we were surrounded by the beautiful bay and islands of the estuary of Parati. Breakfast was with a lot of light banter, and Chico, Marieta and us enjoying last conversation. There was the call to be at the zodiac departure door at 8:00 and all were present. Naturalists double as zodiac hotrodders, so Jack, Buck and Steve were the drivers for the day. I rode in with Chico and crew, the town more beautiful as we drew closer to the quay. And it was on the dock that we made our goodbyes, and thanks from us and from them. (I forgot – Amy had given them a check for $1000 that morning, much appreciated.) Chico was a bit moved, giving me a big abraço, Marieta as well, and vowing to stay in touch with the hope of better times in Brazil and my return. I did the same. They did the final goodbyes (they had arranged rental cars for the drive back to Rio) as I and the naturalists prepared to accompany adventurers on the town tour and then a big lunch at a famous shrimp place we were told about.

Parati is one of the most famous tourist-vacation spots in all Brazil, a beach resort on the coast southeast of Rio and on the border with São Paulo State. Established in 1667 by the Portuguese, it was originally inhabited by the Guaianás Indians, but became important as the end of the "Gold Trail," a rough, cobblestoned road linking Parati port to the gold fields of the interior state to the west in Minas Gerais in the 18th century, a 1200-kilometer road linking the gold fields of Diamantina and Ouro Preto to the coast. The gold once transported to Parati was then moved by ship to Rio and from there exported to Lisbon. Later an overland route direct from Minas to Rio was established and Parati declined, that is, until tourism in the 20th century. Situated in a huge bay with many islands and streams pouring into it, Parati became THE coastal retreat for "Cariocas" as well as "Paulistas" [folks from the huge state of São Paulo]. It is a charming town with colonial architecture, wonderful beaches and fishing and fine restaurants (IA adventurers and staff can vouch for the latter). Incidentally it became known for the best "cachaça" or sugar cane rum in those parts.

A personal aside: upper class friends in Rio encouraged me as a young scholar on a student budget doing research in 1967 to join them on weekends in Parati saying: "It's really a good deal, about $1000 USD for the weekend." That is why my first visit is with AT. Some highlights follow.

The Gold Trail

The naturalists were out on the Gold Trail and checking for animals and birds. The "culture option," my group, started with a long walk, from the long quay, the main plaza with a small band of old retired men playing "cirandinha" music. We saw the small fish market, the cobblestone streets, the beautiful tiled buildings with "azulejos". And there were the churches, a tour with José the local guide; great lunch with some of the adventurers (best shore food on the trip, all kinds of shrimp, etc. icy cold beer). After lunch there was heavy rain and I did a long walk alone to the port; then the unexpected happened. Steve my boss came zooming into the dock in a zodiac with one arm in the air with a pair of crutches and another with an envelope with cash I surmise. "Mike, got to get these to the hospital." So, I walked as fast as my legs would carry me through pouring rain to the port, crossing the river and bridge to the hospital. An adventurer, guess who? Wonky had broken his leg on the slick "Gold Trail" (when it rains, as it had the day before, one imagines slick rocks, no surprise) but was smiling and in good spirits. I talked a bit, delivered the crutches and envelope and walked back to the port. The ride "home" to "Adventurer" was on the zodiac with Buck who zoomed back to the ship while seeing dolphins on the way. Check in, shower, rest. When the news got around everyone agreed Wonky was an okay sort, but, well, Wonky.

So that night the highlight was CC and the up to date tales of Steve, Willie and the naturalists on all the stuff from the last days in Rio and a naturalist hike today in the Atlantic Rain Forest around Parati. It was a bit long with a lot to report. Buck did have luck at the Golden Lion Tamarin Reserve and showed spectacular photos of it all. Steve and Willie had surprises as well – good shots of dolphins in Guanabara Bay and, gulp, three sharks not supposed to be there. Good thing we had no such encounters at the beach. Kelly and Jack showed pictures of the Botanical Gardens and the "Chinese Vista" hike with amazing photos of the animals and birds we had seen. And most recently they talked of the birds and animals around the Gold Trail – parakeets, Toucans, agoutis and our first Capybara.

Dinner was a reprise of sorts for me, time with Leonel and friends, they assuring me that this trip had gone far beyond their expectations, in all respects. We were congratulated particularly for pulling off the Chico Buarque concert, Leonel saying the adventurers would have no idea of that cultural "coup." We talked some of the future, more travel for them, but some surprising suggestions. Leonel said the more he heard from me, and knew there was more to come, that I should not "be wasting my time" in the great "sertão" [a Brazilian term for the backlands of their interior, but meaning a bit of a cultural "out back" for the U.S.] of Nebraska. I should endeavor to join the U.S. State Department. He could help with a strong suggestion to them to "cut bureaucratic red tape" and that I would be welcomed as a cultural attaché in Brazil. That idea had been proposed before, by girlfriend and "siren" Sônia in Rio last year. I told them a bit about her, the Rodrigues Ltd. connection. Leonel wondered did I give it any thought? "No, I could not see anything serious with her, at least at the time, but hell if I know what the future holds."

The next few days all would return to "at sea" routine, adventurers looking forward to resting and more education from the naturalists and cultural speakers. It would be a little over two days to our final stop at the port of Rio Grande in the southernmost state of Brazil, Rio Grande do Sul, and we hoped the high point of Brazilian nature – the TAIM CHICO MENDES RESERVE inland an hour or two. I'll tell a bit of those days, the talks and what surprises the South Atlantic off the coast of southern Brazil held in store.

29

AT SEA WISDOM

July 23rd After a leisurely breakfast Steve asked Harry "to dust off" some of his best, and first was an amazing story of the discovery and then competition and rivalry for colonization of Southern Brazil, Uruguay and Argentina. The Portuguese and the Spaniards would vie for hegemony, contesting southern Brazil (Rio Grande do Sul State today, the Mission territory of the Jesuits there and near Iguaçu on the border with Paraguay and Argentina). Harry, a good Anglican, told of English Protestant Missionaries and Welsh colonies in the entire area. He linked it all to a review of the slave trade in the entire region.

We would finally show one of my all-time favorites "The Mission" that night in the lounge, more when we come to it.

Jack followed in the a.m. with a preview of what we might see during the three days, birds of the South Atlantic. There were the Masked Boobies after the flying fish in the front wake of the ship, and now beginning to see the Petrels, Shearwaters, and the big treat, Black Browed Albatross, one of the largest sea birds on the planet. And Jack even thought we spied our first Arctic Term, a little far north at this point, but there it was.

In the p.m. as promised Steve encouraged me to talk once again of Brazilian Culture, in this case what I knew most and best – Brazil's Folk – Popular Poetry or the "Literatura de Cordel."

I explained once again my research topic of Brazil's folk-popular, narrative poetry (it tells stories) "cordel" and showed images of the covers. There were many positive comments, and several wanted my small English-Portuguese Anthology. Steve praised the talk, once again adding how much I had added to the trip! (Incidentally adventurers liked the handouts; no one else used them on the trip, but several said they would read and use for reference at home. This was a carryover from professorial days in classes – the obligatory summary of the lecture.)

Summary of Notes on the "Literatura de Cordel"

1. Folk-Popular Poetry (narrative) in chapbooks or pamphlets. They tell a story.
2. Came from Portugal in the 18th century, also France, Spain, Italy.
3. In Prose to the Northeast; converted to poetry by the folk-popular poets Entertainment/ teaching/ news.
4. 100,000 titles by end of the 20th century; some have sold one million copies.
5. Sold in markets, fairs, sung by poets, influenced major Brazilian writers, movies, "telenovelas."
6. Show my book: "A Bilingual Anthology of Brazil's Folk – Popular Poetry: English-Portuguese."
7. The big story of "cordel" is in a new book: "Portrait of Brazil in the 20th Century: The Universe of the 'Literatura de Cordel'." (The book goes "live" at Trafford and Amazon shortly after this trip.)
8. Orange business cards not to advertise but to see a good example of the Brazilian woodcut which decorates the covers.

So, the book tells of "Cordel" - a Brazilian Folk-Popular Epic in Ten Chapters or "Cantos."

1. In this we believe
2. The manifestations
3. What not to do: the wages of sin

4. Our heroes
5. Life is a struggle; life is a saga
6. We have our distractions
7. In politics we trust but do not believe
8. There is a big world out there
9. Life is getting difficult
10. This is not the end.

And it wasn't.

That night after dinner we showed "The Mission" in the lounge (but it also went to the TVs in the rooms) with its story of the Jesuit Missions in Southern Brazil and their battle to protect the Indians and themselves from the edict of exile. One must take the Hollywood "extras" which were all fun, but the scene of Robert de Niro climbing up the Iguaçu Falls, the forest and beautiful mission scenes were appreciated by all. It turns out there was no need to stay after the movie but I did do a five - minute introduction.

30

ALL THAT'S ABOVE AND BELOW

July 24th Second Day at Sea after Parati.

Before breakfast I probably had my best conversations with the naturalists all gathered for early morning coffee. They told their stories, where they were from and how they learned their trade and the times on the trips for AT all over the world. Amy was there, much relieved about the flurry of Rio and only one major stop to come and not much to organize – the procedure at the huge commercial port of Rio Grande and the bus to the TAIM resort. "Adventurer" would top off on fuel and we would head back up the coast one – half day to the capital large city of Porto Alegre where adventurers who were not heading on across the sea to South Africa and "The Portuguese Route of Discovery in Asia" would disembark.

Breakfast was intentionally with some adventurers I had not met yet, Canadians from Victoria, B.C. They told of all the birds and wild life on the Island and the shores of B.C., stuff I had never seen but that sounded exciting – whales, eagles, all kinds of sea birds gathered by the hundreds of thousands on the sea rocks. Wow! This was their first time to Brazil and they had all dreamed of the tropics. They loved all the places we had seen and the culture! Xangô back in Recife maybe being the most memorable!

Being a "sort of cultural director," I was honored by Steve to give the last talk – fitting I think – "An Overview of Brazil." It combined what we had seen – Manaus, Belém, Recife, Salvador, Rio, Parati and Rio Grande – with cultural highlights of my research in Brazil, much coming from "Adventures of a 'Gringo' Researcher in Brazil in the 1960." The latter featured images of other places in Brazil to perhaps whet the appetites of the adventurers of what an inland trip in Brazil might bring – the capital Brasília, the trip on a sternwheeler on the São Francisco River, the colonial sights of Minas Gerais, and Iguaçu Falls.

In all humility there was applause by all, even a standing ovation for work well done. I was humbled and moved, not the least by a surprise from Amy – she came up, gave me a kiss in front of everyone and said that AT had truly made a great discovery in the "outback" of Nebraska! Laughter from all. Many came up, shook hands or gave an embrace, some saying their best trip ever on AT!

That p.m. I had that final promised moment with Harry Downing, the two of us alone up in the ship's library. He confided in me (that is the word) that he was thinking of retirement and soon, perhaps after this year's "season." Then my jaw dropped; he said that these past thirty days had shown him that I, Mike Gaherty and college professor, only one-time AT cultural lecturer, would be a good candidate to succeed him, albeit for the New World (his term) and perhaps Spain and Portugal. He said AT could easily arrange that; there were others who could handle the rest of the planet. It could be arranged comfortably as a summer time "gig" allowing me to continue at that outback university in the States! Laughter. He was quite prepared to forward his idea to Susan in personnel should I be open to the idea. That "humbled" me. "Harry, you have just made me feel truly happy and satisfied that this trip was a good decision. I'm overwhelmed and think some quiet time for reflection back in Lincoln is definitely needed, but I thank you and you will be the first to know come the end of Fall Semester. I will share a good scotch drink with you at cocktails and toast the friendship." He said maybe two and would forward to it.

That night videographer Reynaldo promised a "great show" with the second half video of the trip. He would not include TAIM, regrettably, because he would be editing the trip to have VHS tapes ready for everyone before departure.

31

❖────◆────❖

BIRDS, ANIMALS AND THE REST

July 25th. "Adventurer" pulled into the Rio Grande port in early morning rain; we all loaded up for the last big nature phase of the trip, fittingly, I think. The port surprised us – perhaps the largest in Brazil for exportation of soy products, beef, and a major terminal for refitting of the huge open sea oil exploration platforms. The ship would top off on fuel for the quick return to Porto Alegre and the end of the trip, the last day, or partial day, at sea. Tonight would be Captain Tony's and AT's last dinner, meaning Italian wine and last time for reminiscing and conversation. I haven't mentioned purser Joana Oliveira much, but she has handled all paper work and now would prepare the up to date account amounts to be settled tomorrow morning and disembarking papers. Amy would handle disembarkation instructions. Incidentally AT had provided for a post-trip excursion from Porto Alegre to Iguaçu Falls, a sight not to be missed.

We had to await the buses, maybe a one hour delay but not all bad; we saw the impressive activity of the port alongside – rows and rows of Brazil's version of 18 wheelers full of soy for the ships, one huge oil platform in for refurbishing, and many colorful birds on the mooring lines. The buses arrived and we did the two-hour drive to TAIM. It was the first and only chance to see Brazil's "pampas" - rain soaked flat field after field of pastures with … Black Angus! … (almost all the cattle I had seen in northeastern Brazil were "Zebu" or "Brahma" stock) and many birds

Jack the veteran would point out on the way. For those departing the ship at Porto Alegre there would be a chance to see a real Brazilian "gaúcho" dance and music show at what they call the "Galpão." I hoped to see it before my own flight the next a.m. to Atlanta, picking up the international flight in Rio.

TAIM did not disappoint. Officially called the TAIM Ecological Station and run by the Institute for Biodiversity, it consisted in lagoons, swamps, and grasslands living up to its name – the most diverse we had seen. Jumping to the end and the best, Jack, Kelly, and Buck said they may have broken a record – more than 100 species sightings in one day! I can't even begin to remember their list but it included sea birds, lagoon birds and pasture birds as well as some interesting Brazilian "critters."

And just an aside, we saw the largest fica tree ever!

The Enormous Fica Tree at TAIM

Mama Capybara Nursing Baby

Brazilian "Jacaré" – Alligator

I think I spotted our first capybaras – a female nursing her baby – on the road going in. It would be the first of dozens. There were Brazilian alligators (remember "fazendo jacaré" or body surfing in Rio – the local name was the "broad sided caiman)". It was not the same as the famous "pantanal" to the west but for sure was a close second! Bromelia, cactus, and water hyacinths kept Kelly busy and happy. Ibis, herons, flycatchers and my favorite – the Vermillion Flycatcher which, can you believe it, migrates all the way to Arizona in the U.S. For me, a culture specialist, it truly topped off my trip being able to see the nature one dreams of when thinking of Brazil. Maybe I looked a bit like a naturalist with mud boots, IA hat and shirt. Nah.

We returned in mid – p.m. (birds resting), everyone cleaned up from the muddy trails and wading through water (in boots supplied by the ship) and got ready for our last CC and Captain's dinner, to sea in the morning and the half-day to Porto Alegre. All was a bit emotional, the good cheer and final speeches (some too long) by naturalists, Steve and Amy, and Captain Tony himself. All went to their rooms early doing the daunting task of final packing and ready for departure tomorrow.

Then came the surprise.

32

A GLITCH OF SORTS

July 26th. The announcement came mid – morning just an hour out of Rio Grande. Most of us had noticed diminishing speed of the ship, and then no forward progress at all, "Adventurer" with its advanced stabilizer system rolling in the swells. An emergency intercom call came from Captain Tony:

> Adventurers and Staff: Both engines are seized. We suspect fuel contamination. Seasick pills are available at administration. An SOS has been sent. There is a Brazilian Naval Destroyer in the neighborhood, fortunately. They will arrive to tow us into Porto Alegre but in four to five hours. Hang on; this will end well. Emergency generators are now functioning and will take care of AC, water needs. I suggest minimal activity, do NOT look out the windows, perhaps a good time to write the rest of the trip diary! You are in good hands.

I do believe it may have been the longest four hours of my life, maybe for all of us. As long as I didn't move too fast or look outside at the waves, I was able to hold it in check. I'm afraid that was not the case for everyone. Spanish poet García Lorca has a famous poem with this line "Verde, te quiero, verde." ["Green, I love you, Green."] I don't know exactly what he was thinking of, maybe a gypsy lover, or olives in Southern Spain, but in

1929 he was certainly not thinking of us. Veteran adventurers and most staff, not me, had experienced such difficulties before, but this was a new one. Obviously, the main conversation was "How did this happen?" In just two hours (they must have gone "full speed ahead") the destroyer arrived and there was a very efficient hook up, two lines hooked to the bow of "Adventurer" and we felt the ship move again. Most everyone went to the observation decks to witness and photograph this not to be repeated event.

We would find out a little more six hours later when we docked in Porto Alegre and were met by all kinds of big time Naval Officials in uniform. They sent enlisted men to help IA take passengers to a comfortable waiting room, download luggage as planned, and we were all set up in Porto Alegre's most comfortable hotel. We however were not privy to the conversation between Captain Tony and local officials, at least not then.

The good news was that special arrangements were made and all of us were invited to that "Galpão" gaúcho restaurant I talked of earlier for wine, beer and "churrasco" and wonderful music and dancing. Courtesy of the Brazilian government. Most everyone had recovered and took them up on the offer. It was the best of Brazilian "churrasco" together with huge plates of real, tasty fresh tomatoes and lettuce salad, and that icy "Brahma Choppe" beer. And the entertainment was different from anything we had seen in Brazil – girls looking more like Spaniards or Mexicans in colorful dresses dancing with "gaúcho" guys in "bombachas" [long ballooning pants] with big leather belts with daggers and high leather boots – plus gaucho music featuring the accordion. Girls and guys in the same costumes has waited on us. A fitting "final" dinner for adventurers and all of us in Brazil.

Amy had sat beside me and I joined her in her room that evening. We had time to discuss it – "Where do we go from here?" There were some intimate moments and we decided to let things settle down at home in Lincoln for me and see AT's plans for Amy the rest of the year and next. She said she was due for some down time and rest, particularly after this trip. We talked of a reunion back home. She had to get back on the phones and double check departures for the next day, a headache. There actually were few hitches the following morning because Amy had spent time burning the midnight oil earlier in the week, finalizing travel plans that had been set for that day anyway, reservations made and we had the green light to proceed. There was another announcement at breakfast by a Brazilian Naval officer with a full-dress jacket of medals:

> "Adventurer's" fuel tanks have been drained, cleaned and filled with what we assure you is clean diesel fuel from our Naval station and all engine fuel filters replaced. There is no official word or reason yet as to those responsible for your "misfortune," but working in conjunction with the Brazilian Department of Public Security we have learned that three individuals have been apprehended, arrested and subjected to interrogation, suspected leftists for sure! Brazilian internal security will soon 'ferret out the story.' (My editorial interjection to myself – heavy handed for sure!) We apologize, thank you for your cooperation and assure you that Brazil has both welcomed and appreciated your stay the past thirty days."

During that day adventurers not continuing on board were whisked to the airport with flights to Rio and then connecting flights to wherever their international destination might be. Goodbyes were done at the hotel, but sporadic because of different departure times. A different mindset goes into place – the saga of getting home! Real goodbyes and appreciation had taken place on board or at the Gaúcho show. I had talked with Captain Tony, Exec Martim, Purser Joana and Thai guys and girls, expressing my thanks. My last contact was Steve who expressed wholehearted satisfaction for the trip – a huge success from AT and IA point of view, in spite of the one final glitch, and once again how much I had added to the trip. "We could not have done it without you. Will you consider a repeat when we do Brazil again?" I said I would have to rest up in Lincoln and ponder the matter but would never forget this last month and was grateful to AT and IA. "Adventurer" was headed east across the Atlantic to continue the next trip of "The Portuguese Route of Exploration" around South Africa and on over to Goa, and on to Macau. Harry would be "cultural leader" and in great style! Then it would begin its South Pacific turn and eventually, someday, reach home in "O Porto" for refitting.

EPILOGUE

All staff and adventurers received an air mail registered letter from AT ten days later. The three men apprehended in Porto Alegre after interrogation admitted to being members of ARB (Brazilian Revolutionary Action) a small but extreme splinter group of the Brazilian Left. In "Letters" two years ago I wrote of a near kidnapping – of me! – on the way to the Galeão International Airport in Rio, but saved by the SNI, Brazil's FBI, utilizing an undercover armed escort to the airport (revealed to me only later was SNI's motive: to avoid yet another embarrassment to Brazil of a kidnapping of a foreign official or citizen by the Left). I could only surmise how the information was "ferreted out" in Porto Alegre, but had a good idea. I think most adventurers, after the fact, had another story to tell family and friends, and maybe grandchildren!

The above was in conjunction with two phone calls, one from Steve and a second from Amy, both from the ship - shore long-line phone from Macau!

Steve's first: he spoke ever so briefly of the ARB news saying he was confident IA would have no more troubles. He had talked to Harry, and independently of that he wanted to know if I had given consideration to the offer to hire on once again with AT in the future. I could only say, not yet, still settling down for Fall Term and I wanted it to all percolate for a while. I said I was flattered and it would indeed be an honor and a pleasure to repeat "sometime" in the future.

Now Amy. "I've missed you. The naturalists are hitting on me again, but to no avail! Not the same. This has to be short. I've got time off next month and can arrange for a post – trip 'whatchamacallit' – a nice talk with Susan in Los Angeles and some time for us to see if this was just one of those "shipboard romances." What do you say? We make a good team."

My end of the conversation: "Hello Amy, things are busy here, but something's missing, IA routine, that great trip, but mainly our times. You're on for October! Call me when you are off the ship (after a Pacific crossing from Macau) and we can set it up. I like 'whatchamacallits.'"

It happened.

ABOUT THE AUTHOR

Mark Curran is a retired professor from Arizona State University where he worked from 1968 to 2011. He taught Spanish and Portuguese and their respective cultures. His research specialty was Brazil and its "popular literature in verse" or the "Literatura de Cordel," and he has published many articles in research reviews and now some sixteen books related to the "Cordel" in Brazil, the United States and Spain. Other books done during retirement are of either an autobiographic nature – "The Farm" or "Coming of Age with the Jesuits" - or reflect classes taught at ASU on Luso-Brazilian Civilization, Latin American Civilization or Spanish Civilization. The latter are in the series "Stories I Told My Students:" books on Brazil, Colombia, Guatemala, Mexico, Portugal and Spain. "Letters from Brazil I, II, and III" is an experiment combining reporting and fiction. "A Professor Takes to the Sea I and II" is a chronicle of a retirement adventure with Lindblad Expeditions - National Geographic Explorer. "Rural Odyssey – Living Can Be Dangerous" is "The Farm" largely made fiction. "A Rural Odyssey II – Abilene – Digging Deeper" is a continuation of "Rural Odyssey." Now, "Around Brazil on the 'International Adventurer' – A Fictional Panegryic" tells of an expedition in better and happier times in Brazil.

Published Books

A Literatura de Cordel. Brasil. 1973

Jorge Amado e a Literatura de Cordel. Brasil. 1981

A Presença de Rodolfo Coelho Cavalcante na Moderna Literatura de Cordel. Brasil. 1987

La Literatura de Cordel – Antología Bilingüe – Español y Portugués. España. 1990

Cuíca de Santo Amaro Poeta-Repórter da Bahia. Brasil. 1991

História do Brasil em Cordel. Brasil. 1998

Cuíca de Santo Amaro – Controvérsia no Cordel. Brasil. 2000

Brazil's Folk-Popular Poetry – "a Literatura de Cordel" – a Bilingual Anthology in English and Portuguese. USA. 2010

The Farm – Growing Up in Abilene, Kansas, in the 1940s and the 1950s. USA. 2010

Retrato do Brasil em Cordel. Brasil. 2011

Coming of Age with the Jesuits. USA. 2012

Peripécias de um Pesquisador "Gringo" no Brasil nos Anos 1960 ou 'A Cata de Cordel" USA. 2012

Adventures of a 'Gringo' Researcher in Brazil in the 1960s or In Search of Cordel. USA. 2012

A Trip to Colombia – Highlights of Its Spanish Colonial Heritage. USA. 2013

Travel, Research and Teaching in Guatemala and Mexico – In Quest of the Pre-Columbian Heritage

> Volume I – Guatemala. 2013
> Volume II – Mexico. USA. 2013

A Portrait of Brazil in the Twentieth Century – The Universe of the "Literatura de Cordel." USA. 2013

Fifty Years of Research on Brazil – A Photographic Journey. USA. 2013

Relembrando - A Velha Literatura de Cordel e a Voz dos Poetas. USA. 2014

Aconteceu no Brasil – Crônicas de um Pesquisador Norte Americano no Brasil II, USA. 2015

It Happened in Brazil – Chronicles of a North American Researcher in Brazil II. USA, 2015

Diário de um Pesquisador Norte-Americano no Brasil III. USA, 2016

Diary of a North American Researcher in Brazil III. USA, 2016

Letters from Brazil. A Cultural-Historical Narrative Made Fiction. USA 2017.

A Professor Takes to the Sea – Learning the Ropes on the National Geographic Explorer.

> Volume I, "Epic South America" 2013 USA, 2018.
> Volume II, 2014 and "Atlantic Odyssey 108" 2016, USA, 2018

Letters from Brazil II – Research, Romance and Dark Days Ahead. USA, 2019.

A Rural Odyssey – Living Can Be Dangerous. USA, 2019.

Letters from Brazil III – From Glad Times to Sad Times. USA, 2019.

A Rural Odyssey II – Abilene – Digging Deeper. USA, 2020

Around Brazil on the "International Adventurer" – A Fictional Panegyric, USA, 2020

Professor Curran lives in Mesa, Arizona, and spends part of the year in Colorado. He is married to Keah Runshang Curran and they have one daughter Kathleen who lives in Albuquerque, New Mexico, married to teacher Courtney Hinman in 2018. Her documentary film "Greening the Revolution" was presented most recently in the Sonoma Film Festival in California, this after other festivals in Milan, Italy and New York City. Katie was named best female director in the Oaxaca Film Festival in Mexico.

The author's e-mail address is: profmark@asu.edu
His website address is: www.currancordelconnection.com

Printed in the United States
By Bookmasters